BAYOU'S LAMENT

BAYOU'S LAMENT

A LABYRINTH OF SOULS NOVEL

BY

CHERYL OWEN-WILSON

ShadowSpinners Press

To my husband, Jay Wilson, for his unwavering encouragement of my many artistic endeavors. Thank you for always being there to support our large family, and for giving up our Sunday adventures so I could follow the voices of *Bayou's Lament* to conclusion.

Acknowledgements

Many thanks must go out in the creation of this book. First and foremost to Elizabeth Engstrom. Without her friendship, ever-ready words of wisdom, and introduction to the tribe of writers I now call friends, the voices in my head would never have seen themselves placed on the page. To Christina Lay, editor and publisher extraordinaire, who once said, "I want to be the first to publish one of Cheryl's stories." I hope she knows those words carried me far. To Hilery Kirkman, daughter and fellow writer, thanks for listening and helping when I couldn't find my way out of the labyrinth of my mind. To Matthew Lowes for the hours spent in editing at my dining room table, and being the mastermind behind the Labyrinth of Souls game. And last but certainly not least, to the Ghost Story Weekend gang, going strong at twenty-plus years, and to my writing group the Inklings.

Editor's Preface

Dungeon Solitaire: Labyrinth of Souls is a fantasy game for tarot cards, written by Matthew Lowes and Illustrated by Josephe Vandel. In the game you defeat monsters, disarm traps, open doors, and explore mazes as you delve the depths of a dangerous dungeon. Along the way you collect treasure and magic items, gain skills, and gather companions.

Now ShadowSpinners Press is publishing this and other stand-alone novels inspired by the game. Each *Labyrinth of Souls* novel features a journey into a unique vision of the underworld.

The Labyrinth of Souls is more than an ancient ruin filled with monsters, trapped treasure, and the lost tombs of bygone kings. It is a manifestation of a mythic underworld, existing at a crossroads between people and cultures, between time and space, between the physical world and the deepest reaches of the psyche. It is a dark mirror held up to human experience, in which you may find your dreams … or your doom. Entrances to this realm can appear in any time period, in any location. There are innumerable reasons why a person may enter, but it is a place antagonistic to those who do, a place where monsters dwell, with obstacles and illusions to waylay adventurers, and whose very walls can be a force of corruption. It is a haunted place, ever at the edge of sanity.

Editor's Preface

Dungeon Solitaire: Labyrinth of Souls is a fantasy game for tarot cards, written by Matthew Lowes and Illustrated by Josephe Vandel. In the game you defeat monsters, disarm traps, open doors, and explore mazes as you delve the depths of a dangerous dungeon. Along the way you collect treasure and magic items, gain skills, and gather companions.

Now ShadowSpinners Press is publishing this and other stand-alone novels inspired by the game. Each *Labyrinth of Souls* novel features a journey into a unique vision of the underworld.

The Labyrinth of Souls is more than an ancient ruin filled with monsters, trapped treasure, and the lost tombs of bygone kings. It is a manifestation of a mythic underworld, existing at a crossroads between people and cultures, between time and space, between the physical world and the deepest reaches of the psyche. It is a dark mirror held up to human experience, in which you may find your dreams … or your doom. Entrances to this realm can appear in any time period, in any location. There are innumerable reasons why a person may enter, but it is a place antagonistic to those who do, a place where monsters dwell, with obstacles and illusions to waylay adventurers, and whose very walls can be a force of corruption. It is a haunted place, ever at the edge of sanity.

BAYOU'S LAMENT

The creatures that visited my every nightmare existed as myth within the shadowed bayou world of my mother and her kind. I would be way past my youth before I'd once again walk the swampy Island of my childhood. There I would be carried down into the depths of hell. For where myth resides, there is also truth.

—Diary of Veya Marie St. James, PhD

Chapter One

She sat slumped on cold, metal stairs struggling for breath. With each labored inhale an old familiar scent filled her senses, the stagnant stench of decay. She sat between the fourth and fifth floors of her office building in a stairwell she'd traversed hundreds of times. Yet, she could not shake the feeling she'd been transported through a time warp back to her childhood and the nightmares it held.

Invisible rubber bands tightened and pulsed across her chest. Panic attacks had always walked hand in hand with her childhood memories. Memories she—Veya Marie St. James—had eradicated within the first year of leaving the place where they'd originated. The Island, the home of her birth, hidden deep within southern Louisiana's swamplands. A land fed by layer upon layer of decomposing foliage and dead animals resulting in the odor now assaulting her senses.

Veya had been eighteen when she left the Island. She was now a thirty-nine-year-old woman with a nineteen-year-old daughter.

The sensation of having no control over her own body diminished with each breath, until she could sit upright without the fear of her chest being crushed by an unseen vice.

A panic attack after so many years. Why?

She searched the stairwell for the kid who'd just scared the hell out of her. *It was a kid, wasn't it?* She'd been fumbling in her purse for her phone thinking she should call to check on her daughter, Triste. When she'd looked up, he'd been standing in her way, a four-foot tall black goblin with pointy ears, a tail, and red glowing slits for eyes. It's the end of August, not October, she'd thought right before her phone fell from her hand, and her body began its well-tuned dance with the all-consuming panic. An affliction it had taken her months in therapy to overcome.

She called out, "Where the hell are you, you little cretin?" When no answer came, she wearily climbed the steps out of the stairwell, careful to avoid looking in its dark corners.

Costumes these days are too realistic.

⬥

The image of the kid with glistening red eyes followed her through her first appointment. Mrs. Branson was one of her many patients filled with delusional beliefs of their dead loved ones contacting, or even protecting them, from the great beyond.

Veya absently listened as the woman once again recounted her dead husband Norman's many virtues. Her mind couldn't let go of the incident in the stairwell, and it overlapped with the phone conversation she'd had with her daughter that morning.

"I'm fine Mom. Really. I promise I'll be at my classes tomorrow. It's my second year of college, no big deal to miss a few classes. I just need to lay low today, burrow in my *gray* and by tomorrow all will be bright and shiny." Even as Triste tried to reassure her, Veya knew her daughter was attempting to swallow tears when she'd spoken.

She cringed at Triste's reference to *gray*, the euphemism, or code word they'd settled on when discussing Triste's recent fog of depression. Her daughter had always been filled with such a positive energy, at times Veya thought she could actually feel happiness radiate from her body. But over the past months Triste had been invaded by a sadness Veya couldn't comprehend.

When Triste said, "Since I know you're going to ask, yes I took my pill this morning," Veya knew her daughter wanted to cut the call short, so their conversation had ended before she could tell Triste that perhaps she should increase her dosage.

Mrs. Branson's voice cut through Veya's thoughts. "Dr. St. James? I know your strong opinions on a world beyond the one we live in. But how do you explain Norman's voice speaking to me clear as day when I put the necklace on?"

Veya, pulled from her own thoughts, responded, "Mrs. Branson, can you please repeat your question?"

"I've told you time and again to call me Delilah."

"Sorry, but you're Mrs. Branson to me. Chalk it up to my southern upbringing. It's an unfortunate habit. I automatically refer to any female even slightly older as Miss or Missus." The very idea of anything from her childhood having sway over Veya as an adult twisted knots in her already nervous stomach. She said, "Please continue, Delilah".

"I was saying, I know why I started seeing you in the first place. To move beyond what you've diagnosed as my unhealthy beliefs after my husband's death. But my finding the necklace can't be a coincidence, can it? I've turned my house upside down since Norman's death looking for it. Then on the one-year anniversary of his accident I find it hanging from the edge of the photo I keep of him on my nightstand!"

Delilah caressed the oval hematite stone encircled by diamonds dangling from her neck and held it out for Veya to do the same while saying, "Look, isn't it beautiful?"

Veya flinched, her heartbeat increased. She hoped her movement and apprehension at the sight of the stone hadn't been noticed by Mrs. Branson. Clearing her throat, she spoke in her usual, analytical, monotone voice, "Mrs.—excuse me, Delilah—while I understand a person's desire to believe their dearly departed is shielding them from harm, I also understand the psychological damage they can suffer if they carry this belief to an extreme."

She looked at her notepad rather than watch the woman's fingers still clasped around the stone.

"But I know he was there. In the room when I found the necklace. I think he's waiting for me to join him."

Veya suppressed her concern and wrote *suicidal.* "What do you mean? Are you considering harming yourself Mrs. … Delilah?"

The woman looked at her as though she were the delusional one. "No, of course not. Why would you even think such a thing? I only meant, he'll be waiting for me when the time comes. I … I think it's protecting me." She again held out the necklace toward Veya.

Stones! What would Mrs. Branson think if she knew my history with stones, my Mother's stones? Veya's hand reached to move aside a phantom rawhide string rubbing against her skin. Even though it hadn't been there since she'd been nine years old, at times she could still feel the rough leather scratching at the base of her skull, as though trying to burrow under her skin. No rawhide string. What she felt instead was the clasp of a silver chain holding the pendant she'd worn since her grandmamma's death. Its presence gave her a sense of calm.

She shifted in her overstuffed chair. The irony of her next question was not completely lost to her. She asked,

"How can an object be protecting you? What proof do you have?" The room had warmed.

Delilah sat up straighter. Her eyes widened and she spoke with a defiance-laced voice. "I went to get the mail yesterday and a car barely missed me. I know you'll think I'm … I heard a voice telling me to be careful. The voice was Norman's."

Veya wrote, *Research side effects of delusional meds in women over seventy.* She said, "Have you spoken to your housekeeper, asked if she discovered the necklace she knew you'd been searching for? Perhaps she placed it as a surprise for you?"

Confusion etched Delilah's face as she responded. "No, I haven't. Never even occurred to me."

Veya's phone vibrated indicating the end of the session. Mrs. Branson stood. Veya didn't. The woman's newly found stone glinted inches from Veya's face—toxic—pulling at her carefully buried memories. Her chest tightened and her anxiety escaped in caustic words aimed at her patient, "Mrs. Branson don't put your faith in a stone. I mean sentimental items. This supernatural power you're giving this thing is an illusion that can be dangerous. I would advise against such thoughts for your continued mental health. I suggest you take the necklace off and move on with your life."

Mrs. Branson spoke in a whisper behind the hand clasped over her mouth in shock. Her other hand held the necklace. "Delilah, remember?"

Veya had never before spoken so harshly to a patient.

"Yes, Delilah. My apologies. I may have presented my opinion in too severe a manner." She recovered her clinical tone and continued. "I think given your current … well, we shouldn't wait another month for your regularly scheduled session. On your way out, please ask Denise at reception to get you in next week."

Delilah's red-rimmed eyes were narrow slits staring back at Veya as she left the room.

The rest of Veya's day went as always, scheduled to the second with patients and compiling clinical papers for publication. Well known in her chosen field of Abnormal Psychology, she lived and breathed her work.

Dusk entered through her office window by the time she'd completed and emailed her latest study. The clinical trial contained a group of thirty volunteers, and served as the cornerstone of a behavioral therapy she'd created. Each of the participants had previously been diagnosed with various psychoses involving an acceptance of the supernatural. In each and every case she'd assisted the volunteer in re-patterning their irrational beliefs. She intended to use the process to develop a new method of therapy for future patients with similar belief patterns.

After calling Triste several times with no response and leaving numerous "please call me, no matter how late" messages, she left her office. The morning's panic in the stairwell shadowed her worry over Triste. Where had her sunny, smiling daughter disappeared to, and who was the nineteen-year-old woman of gloom masquerading in her stead?

Every instinct Veya possessed told her to go to her daughter's apartment to check on her wellbeing. But she knew Triste hated her overprotective interferences. Unable to shake her apprehension, she reached for the comfort of statistical reassurance. The latest regimen of meds combined with talk and behavioral therapies were working. Until the morning's conversation, Veya hadn't heard the melancholy in her daughter's voice for several weeks. *A minor setback, a small increase in Triste's meds and she'll be back on track.*

Pleased to have another clinical study complete she decided not to go to her empty home, but instead to treat herself to dinner out.

She chose the elevator as opposed to her normal routine of taking the stairs. Looking down at her sensible brown work flats and wishing she'd put a pair of heels in her car, a glint on the carpeted floor caught her eye. For a stuttered heartbeat she thought Mrs. Branson had lost the stone in her necklace. Repulsed, she kicked the offending thing with the tip of her shoe only to find it was an empty candy wrapper. Still, a shiver of cold fingers draped themselves around her neck as she left the elevator and walked briskly to her car.

She'd decided on Italian by the time she exited the underground garage. Madonna's *Like a Prayer* blasted from the radio. She changed the station. Thinking of Mrs. Branson, she spoke to the radio, "Sorry Madonna, but life is not a mystery. Life is what you make of it. Work hard, plan ahead."

She flipped the car's visor down to check her makeup in its mirror. Her shoulder length, bottle-dyed—because her natural black hair made her see her mother every time she looked in a mirror—blond hair and blue eyes were a sharp contrast to the photo of a curly, red-headed, green-eyed, two-year-old Triste attached to the visor. When she flipped the visor back up the photo fell from the clip and onto the passenger's seat. *Triste.*

Her daughter had been the *only* thing not planned in Veya's life. Two years after leaving home for college, a brief affair with her English Lit professor had created Triste. He'd been recently divorced and everything she'd always dreamed of in a man: intelligent, gorgeous, and of course, logical. Unfortunately, his brain also led him to believe it perfectly reasonable to sleep with other young, naïve, willing female students in his classes.

"Had to make up for lost time," he'd told her. By the time she realized she was pregnant, he'd been fired and she never tried to find him.

The idea of running back to the place she'd left, her family, the Island, had never entered her mind. Guilt at times plagued her. Triste knew nothing of her grandparents or her Aunt Brin, Veya's younger sister and only living sibling. All Triste knew about her mother's family history was that she'd grown up in Louisiana and had no living family she cared to stay in contact with. Once, Triste had overheard a phone conversation between Veya and Brin. Veya told her daughter Brin was an old high school acquaintance, nothing more. Her lies weighed heavy, but she convinced herself she was doing what was best, protecting Triste. When her daughter tried to pry more from her, she filled the gaps with stories of moving to Oregon and their early years together, mother and daughter on their own.

Triste knew only Ashland as home. Veya accomplished what she wanted for herself, for her daughter. They had a stable, normal life.

The radio blasted, *Born on the Bayou*. She turned the irritating lyrics off and drove in silence to Martino's, her favorite Italian restaurant.

"Hey ya, Veya." Daniel the bartender winked at her as she entered. She asked to be seated outside overlooking the city's main street. Daniel came out to take her order.

"Hi, Daniel. The usual please." She spoke from behind the menu. As he left she pondered. *Why, why did I agree to go out with him and why did I sleep with him on our first date?* She smiled, because there had been no sleeping. *Why is he here? It's his night off.* For over a month she'd avoided his requests for another date using excuses about work.

He returned saying, "So ya got a night off? Ya sure are lookin' mighty fine ta night, darlin'." To avoid looking at him, she watched the passersby on the street below headed to the Shakespeare Festival. But when his spice laden cologne mixed with the smell of the double scotch he'd slid in front of her reached her nose, she looked up.

"I … um, yes, I slipped away for dinner, then back to work." She glanced down and studied the menu she knew by heart. His southern voice alone should've repelled her. Damn those cat green eyes. They pleaded with her. *No, don't listen to his syrupy wooing. So smooth and soothing like his hands roaming … stop!*

Daniel persisted, "I do hope you'll take me up on anotha' date sometime soon, darlin'. We could take in a movie or go for a stroll through the park." He took her hand, placed a kiss on the top, and before she could pull away, he'd turned her hand palm up and placed another on the inside of her wrist. He then sauntered to the table across the room where a woman waved for his attention. Veya's hand tingled with heat where he'd left the soft, wet kisses. *It's loneliness. You'll be fine once you get used to Triste being gone.*

The restaurant filled for the evening and she ate hurriedly. Daniel tried to get her attention; she pretended not to see him.

Leaving the restaurant and faced with an empty home and empty bed, she went to the park hoping the outdoor serenity would calm her jangled nerves, helping her to sleep.

Lithia Park was Veya's favorite place in the town she'd chosen as home. A sense of calm washed over her the farther she strolled through its sycamore trees following the curved path along the creek. She reached her favorite spot, a duck pond nestled in the center of the park and sat on a bench she knew had to be indented with the shape of her body given the number of hours she'd spent there. Summers in shorts, fall and spring in layers and winter wrapped in a warm coat. The park became her refuge from the world, nestled in the cocoon of nature.

Triste had taken her first steps from the bench chasing the birds floating on the pond's surface. "Quack, quack," she'd been saying, in a singsong manner when her chubby little legs tottered those first memorable movements. They'd spent many weekends alone picnicking in the park. There'd been two men over the years that Veya had allowed to meet her daughter. But in the end the relationships had failed. When Triste begged to live on her own at nineteen Veya had in turn pleaded for her to stay, but her daughter had as usual gotten her way.

She pulled out her phone to call Triste. It was 11 p.m. She hesitated, and in the end decided not to call at the risk of waking Mary, Triste's new roommate. The woman, new to town, worked odd hours as an emergency room nurse.

By the time Veya ambled slowly through the canopy of trees toward her car, a full moon played hide and seek between their branches. Her thoughts drifted to her favorite pastime as a child of running crazily between the many trees on the Island where frogs sang out in the swamp and mosquitoes bit at her ankles. A tree branch caught in her hair and the memory fled. The tangled branch pulled her back to the park in Ashland where no mosquitoes danced at her feet, and where the only singing she heard came from a bar a block over.

She threw her jacket in the passenger seat and noticed Triste's picture wasn't there. Searching around and under the seat, she finally looked up. The photo clipped to the visor stared back at her. *Must have put it back before I went to dinner.* Leaving the visor down she placed a kiss on her right index finger and touched it to the photo, then turned on the ignition and drove home.

Within minutes Veya had turned every light on in the house and was dressed for bed. Moving from the bathroom back to her bedroom, her phone rang from its place on her bedside table. *Triste?* She ran the rest of the way, stepping on something sharp in the hallway as she went. The phone had gone to voice message by the time she reached it. Not Triste, but Daniel. She didn't return his call.

With her left foot bleeding, she limped to the bathroom. After placing a Band-Aid over the small cut, she went to investigate what had caused the injury. On the tan carpeted runner in the hallway she found the culprit. She picked up the offending thing only to drop it—a tiny shard of obsidian resembling the hematite Mrs. Branson had so lovingly caressed hours before in her office. *How the hell did this get in here?* She took no time in opening her bedroom window and throwing the stone as far as she could from her sight, and her home.

Foot stinging and lights out, she hoped for sleep. But first her brain searched a logical reason for the obsidian. After many loops around dead ends she settled on Triste's thick-soled black boots. The deep treads would allow a piece of stone to be tracked into the house. Triste shared her mother's love of the outdoors, but it'd been months since they'd been hiking. She'd suggest they go soon. Mystery solved, she fell into a deep sleep only to be woken by her daughter.

"Mom, Mom, wake up. I'm scared, Mamma. Help me. Please help me." Triste stood at the foot of Veya's bed dressed in an ankle length white cotton nightgown. Along its neckline were the tiny pink roses Veya had spent hours embroidering. Triste's knee-length auburn hair whipped around her face like a wind was trying to steal each strand from her head.

"Baby, baby what's the matter? Why are you here in the middle of the night? What scared you?" Veya attempted to clear her mind from its sleep-filled stupor. She tried to lift up from her prone position in bed and reach for her daughter, but found she couldn't move more than her neck to see the end of her bed.

Her arms would not lift to throw the covers from her body.

Her legs would not move themselves over the side of the bed.

I'm paralyzed!

For the second time that day panic clawed at her chest. She strained her neck looking helpless to where Triste stood. A wind she could not feel tore at her daughter, twisting the gown tightly around her rail thin body.

This is a bad dream. A nightmare.

"Mamma where am I? Please help me."

"I'm trying sweetie, I'm trying." *Wake up Veya. Wake up!*

Behind Triste there should've been a wall filled with every picture she'd ever drawn for her mother. Instead there was a trunk of a leafless tree silhouetted against the night sky. The bare limbs reached out toward Triste.

It's a dream, just a dream.

A distinct odor settled around Veya as the realization of where Triste could be came to her. The swamp—stagnant water filled with the heated muck of its underbelly—the very smell she'd labored through in the stairwell of her office building that morning. The stench melded with the overwhelming panic she'd always felt when attempting to retrieve childhood memories.

Triste was on—the Island!

Veya tried in vain, once again, to reach for her daughter, but her body remained paralyzed. She watched unable to move as the branches of the tree reached Triste, pulling and yanking her back. One minute Triste stood at the edge of her bed, the next moment she disappeared into the dark void of a night sky filled with silhouettes of flailing tree limbs.

Veya jerked upright in her bed, covered in sweat. "Triste?" Her phone chimed with the ringtone she'd chosen for Triste's calls. Reaching for her phone, she scanned the bedroom wall. No Triste, no tree limbs; just a colorful wall adorned with her daughter's many drawings.

A dream, just a damn dream.

She was so relieved; she'd forgotten her still ringing phone. With shaking hands she answered it.

"Sweetie, I'm glad you called. What time is it?"

"Miss St. James, Dr. St. James, this is Mary, Triste's roommate. I'm calling about Triste. Her alarm went off twice and I didn't hear her get up so I went to her room to check on her. She was still sleeping. I tried to wake her. But she won't wake up. I checked her vitals. Her breathing is fine not erratic, nor is her heartbeat; I see nothing irregular in anything I've checked. It's as though she's in some kind of coma. I'm so sorry."

"What? Put her on the phone."

"Did you hear what I said? I can't. I've called an ambulance."

Veya heard sirens through the phone telling her either the fire truck, or hopefully both the fire truck and ambulance had arrived at her daughter's apartment.

Oh, dear God. Triste!

"Please stay with her. I'll meet you at the hospital."

She was dressed and running back to her room to get her phone when the smells always preceding her panic bouts hit her again. Then she stepped in a puddle of muddy water at the foot of her bed.

Chapter Two

Veya honked her horn at cars driving too slow and held her breath when red lights lasted too long. Why? Why had she dreamed Triste on the Island? She took the photo of baby Triste from the sun visor. While holding the precious image in her hand, she desperately searched her mind for the protection prayer she'd heard her grandmamma recite. When the words wouldn't surface, she resorted to the more practical task of making a mental note to call about the leaking roof in her bedroom. As though confirming her suspicions, heavy clouds began releasing their burden of autumn rain, drenching her when she left her parked car and entered the hospital.

Bile rose in her throat as she hurried through the glass doors of the sterile building. The place reeked of antiseptic cleansers. She loathed hospitals, with their too bright lights, and stark white walls with disease seeping from every room. It's why she'd chosen to have Triste in a midwife's home. Her daughter had never set foot in a hospital. That is, until this day.

A frail senior citizen stood behind the information desk, looking more like he should've been admitted as a patient. He handed her a map of the hospital, placing a circle around the location of the ER. She walked in the direction of the scarlet sphere. Her trembling hands wrinkled the page, while she tried desperately not to think of what might be transpiring behind the whispers, or occasional whimpers, coming from the half-closed doors of each room she passed.

An overwhelming melancholy stalked her the closer she came to the ER. When the misery overcame her a bone deep despair wrapped tightly, like a heavy blanket filled with worry, around her.

She picked up her pace through the labyrinth of identical hallways in an attempt to rid herself of the burden. Yet with each turn taken, the more constricting the shroud of gloom became.

She thought of her cherished grandmamma who had died in a hospital after being transferred from the care facility where she'd lain in a coma for weeks. Veya had been nine years old when she entered the hospital with her family in search of her grandmamma, her confidant, her friend. The elderly woman's waking from the coma was what prompted the transfer. Veya had been so excited at the prospect of having her grandmamma back. But her grandmamma never came home from the hospital, and her mother's recounting of what happened never matched

Veya's own memory of that day. Veya's mother insisted that by the time they reached the hospital her grandmamma had already died, but Veya remembered quite differently.

Immersed in her sudden, intrusive memory Veya barely missed colliding with an orderly pushing a gurney. The shape of a body covered in a sheet stenciled with the hospital's name lay on it. The sight of the body forced the shadowy recollection of her grandmamma from its hidden confines and her nine-year-old self came back in a flash. Her grandmamma had not been dead when she and her family arrived at the hospital. *Remember*, her younger self pleaded. *Remember Grandmamma come past ya layin' on the bed with wheels on it? Her head be covered in a glowin' white sheet, but her hand reached for ya from under it. Ya heard her callin' out to ya. Her fingers was a'holdin' on ta somethin', wantin' ya ta take it. Ya ran ta her. Mamma yanked ya away. But not 'afore Grandmamma dropped what she be holdin' into your hand, then they rolled her away. They never rolled her back out.*

The *thing* her grandmamma had given her was the pendent she'd touched when conversing with Mrs. Branson. It hung under her blouse, a rectangular brass, filigree-etched watch with a pearlescent face. A sharp contrast to the phantom rope necklace she'd been reminded of in the session with its unpolished crystallized stone. She'd been forced to wear it as a child. The rope necklace had always given her a sense of foreboding, while the feel of the cool metal chain she now wore against her skin combined with the weight of the pendant gave her a sense of calm and serenity. She couldn't recall a time when she'd not seen the watch on her grandmamma's wrist when she was alive. She often wondered if it'd kept time before it was given to her, because the hands never moved after her father had had the watch refashioned as a pendant. The presence of her grandmamma was always there in the few happy memories Veya held of her childhood. *How I wish you were here now.* The pendant warmed against her skin as though saying, *I am.*

She released the memory, but like a sticky cobweb its threads remained, tangled in her concern over Triste. Triste, whom Mary had said was in a coma-like state. Veya wouldn't allow the idea of the two women's illnesses to be connected.

Mary, Triste's roommate, came around a corner just as the ER nurses' station came into Veya's view. She'd met the woman only once, a brief introduction, as Mary left for work.

Veya didn't wait for Mary to reach her. Her voice echoed down the hallway. "Where is she?"

"Dr. St. James, I'm so glad you're here. She's still in the ER. I'm in a waiting room down this way."

"What have they told you? Is she awake now?"

Veya's five-foot nine-inch frame towered over Mary, a petite woman barely over five feet. The tiny woman's blue-black, shoulder length, blunt cut hair accented her olive skin and contrasted starkly with her bright blue eyes. Veya followed her down the hallway realizing she couldn't be more than a few years older than Triste.

The narrow passageway they walked held rooms on either side, reminding Veya of a movie she'd once watched, where the prisoner was forced to march down a barely lit, tiled corridor to his death. *Only this isn't my death waiting at the end, it's Triste's. No! Don't even think it.*

The blanket of unease weighing her down since entering the hospital pushed deeper through her as though being infused and absorbed by her skin. With each step its bulk increased. The usual lightness of her agile 135-pound self disappeared under its heaviness. Simultaneously she envisioned her tall frame inching ever shorter with each laborious stride taken. A few feet in front of her, Mary entered a side room, and sat in a chair near the open door. Veya heaved her worry-laden body onto the sofa opposite the chair.

"Tell me what the paramedics said." She knew her voice sounded harsh, but she had no time for politeness. "Has no one been to talk to you since you got here?"

Mary toyed with a pale blue stone hanging from a silver chain at her neck. "The paramedics really couldn't tell me any more than I've already told you. Triste did tell you I'm an RN here at the hospital?"

Veya nodded and motioned with a wave of her hand for Mary to continue.

"As I told you on the phone, I detected nothing abnormal in her vitals. Her heart rate, blood pressure, and breathing were all within range."

Veya interrupted, "But you couldn't wake her?"

"That's right. As I told you, when she didn't respond to her alarm, I went to her room and found her asleep in her bed. Nothing looked out of place. But she didn't look …" Her eyes narrowed as though puzzling over her response.

"Out with it. What?"

"She didn't look peaceful. You know? Her brow was furrowed."

Veya pictured Triste with her brow pinched. An image she'd seen all too many times in the past months.

Mary continued, "It wasn't only her creased brow, her lips were pursed too. I thought maybe she was having a bad dream. You know she's been having a lot of those? I've been here for six weeks and in that time, they've increased in frequency. So I decided to wake her. But she wouldn't wake up. She just would not wake up!" Mary's words dissolved into silent tears. She pulled a tissue from her purse. "I'm sorry. I should've known. I should've done something before …"

Veya had lost all sense of time since Mary's call and asked, "How long have you been here?" Then seeing the tissue in Mary's hand added, "Don't put this on yourself. I'm thankful you were there to call."

Mary looked down at her watch. "We've been here about an hour now. I'm sure the ER doctor will have answers soon. I checked; Dr. Ming is on duty tonight."

"An hour?" Veya couldn't sit any longer. Someone would answer her questions, or take her to her daughter.

At the nurses' station Veya watched impatiently as the two nurses behind the privacy counter were so deep in whispered conversation, they didn't see her. The younger of the two said, "I think she's a suicide. Too bad, she's so young."

The older, hard-edged woman replied, "Probably a pill popper. After all, she'd have had access to any number of drugs through mommy dearest."

Veya contained her anger by drumming her perfectly manicured nails along the counter's metal surface and chose her words carefully; however, anxiety over Triste caused her words to come out more caustic than she intended. "Since you ladies seem to have nothing to do other than gossip about patients, maybe you can find a doctor to tell me what the hell is going on with my daughter. She's been in the ER for over an hour, and I've not been informed of her status. Her name is Triste Dawn St. James."

The immediate flush sprouting upon the women's faces told Veya they had indeed been discussing Triste.

The younger nurse looked at the chart she held in her hand. "Yes, Ms. St. James, we've been waiting for you. Dr. Ming should be out shortly to speak with you. In the meantime if you could provide us with some form of identification? There's paperwork to be completed."

"It's *Dr.* St. James." She pulled out her wallet and handed the woman her driver's license.

Both nurses disappeared to a back room. A moment later, the younger nurse came out with her license. She handed the card back along with a clipboard filled with forms. Holding her head down, her eyes hooded she said, "I'm sorry about your daughter ma'am. Dr. Ming consults on cases like this throughout the world. I'm also sorry for earlier. It was highly inappropriate."

The woman looked away from Veya toward the hallway.

Veya asked, "What do you mean 'cases like this'?"

"I really can't say more. The doctor will be out shortly. You can take the papers back to the waiting room. Fill them out there." She again entered the back room leaving Veya standing alone.

Veya had barely sat down in the waiting room when a doctor appeared in the doorway.

He extended his hand in greeting while saying, "Dr. St. James, I'm Dr. Ming. I've been attending your daughter. She's currently resting comfortably and in the process of being transferred to a private room in ICU. I know how concerned you must be. Unfortunately, I've not been able to ascertain the cause of her coma-like state. I'm sorry to say, I can't venture a diagnosis until I've studied all the test results. I trust we'll have answers when all the lab work is concluded. I expect it, at the latest, by midday tomorrow."

He looked toward Mary with questioning eyes.

Veya understood his silent inquiry and said, "This is Triste's roommate, an RN here at the hospital. Feel free to speak in front of her. You're still unable to wake Triste?" She couldn't keep the fear from her voice as a heaviness pulled at her from within. *Coma-like?* Even as she struggled not to allow it the thought finally took hold. *Like Grandmamma?*

Without letting him give the positive response mirrored in his eyes, she continued. "But, why? What can cause this?" She pointed toward Mary. "Mary says she found her in bed with no sign of anything disturbed in her room. Could she have fallen earlier in the day, hit her head and not realized the extent of her injury?"

"I've reviewed the X-rays. There's no indication of head trauma or injury to her body, no lacerations, no bruising."

Her body. A cold chill began to tap dance along Veya's arms. *She's not a body. She's a girl and she's still alive!* The words came unbidden, followed by a mental picture of her grandmamma's dead body surrounded in the burgundy silk confines of her open coffin. Dr. Ming's words played like a tape loop in her mind, *Coma-like state.* How often had she heard those exact words whispered when the Islanders tried to shield her young ears from their gossip?

Her grandmamma had lain in a coma-like state for several weeks. Long enough for her to be taken off the Island and placed in the Magnolia Home for the Aged. When she'd abruptly awakened, the doctor at Magnolia had told her parents. "She woke extremely agitated talking nonsense. She kept asking about "the child," but could never tell us what child. When she became violent with the staff, we had to transfer her to the hospital's psych ward for evaluation."

Veya had never understood why her parents had her grandmamma taken off the Island and placed in the Magnolia Home for the *Dying,* which is what the old woman had called it. Why hadn't *they* moved with her? One of many things she held against them.

Her mother and her grandmamma had quarreled often. But their heated words had increased in the days before the elder woman had fallen into a coma. What the arguments were about her mother would never say, even when Veya, no longer a child, had asked repeatedly. Her mother's response had always been the same. "Ya have no interest in the workin's of the Island, Veya. Ya always have made it clear as glass you'd be leavin' as soon as ya was of age. What went on with Mamma and me ya can never understand. So, leave me, and your grandmamma's quarrelin' be."

Veya had overheard fragments of many of the arguments, but one in particular plagued her. Her grandmamma, speaking to her mother had said, "Ya have ta tell her, Marie. Let her make up her own mind. Ya can't force it on her." The remainder of the disagreement had been held behind closed doors, and in hushed whispers Veya couldn't hear. Was the disagreement over her?

Dr. Ming's ice-cold hand brushed against Veya's upper right arm. The touch brought her back to the hospital and to the cold reality of current day. Should she tell him about her grandmamma; could Triste's illness be hereditary? No, she refused to believe anything from the Island could have anything to do with her daughter, and Dr. Ming saved her from making the final decision by broaching a subject that caused all reason to leave Veya's mind.

With caution edged in his voice he asked, "The toxicology tests I requested on your daughter should be back by tomorrow, but I hoped you could give me information on the anti-depressants your colleague Dr. Anderson has prescribed? It being Saturday, we couldn't get anyone other than his service by phone. Do you know of any change in her dosages? The information accessed shows a prescription for an anti-psychotic as well as an anti-depressant. She last refilled the anti-depressant two weeks ago. But the other, she filled only once. Generally that's an indication the patient ceased taking the medication or is not taking the recommended dosage. Could she have …" He paused then continued. "Could she have saved the pills and taken them—"

Veya cut off his words before he could finish. "If you're implying my daughter attempted suicide Dr. Ming, please cross the thought off your list of possible diagnoses. It is not possible. The treatment for her temporary depression has been going quite well."

Triste's melancholy laced voice of the day before floated like a gloomy fog around Veya. That coupled with Dr. Ming's startled face caused Veya to apologize. "Dr. Ming, please forgive my outburst, but my daughter is, well she's …" Veya couldn't say what she was thinking—*she's all I have in this world.*

Dr. Ming turned to leave the room, but before he did, he said, "No need for an apology, I understand. I'll contact you when the lab results come back, or should any new developments occur."

When she returned the clipboard with its completed forms, the younger nurse informed her, "Your daughter is in ICU, room 5B." Veya pulled the wrinkled map from her purse and allowed the nurse to circle 5B in blue ink.

Her legs wouldn't carry her fast enough. She passed the waiting room and told Mary she'd call when she knew more.

In the ICU, a glass-enclosed room held Triste, motionless other than the rise and fall of her chest. The nurse sitting at the station outside the room acknowledged Veya then went back to studying her computer screen. Veya entered the room; her heart had the staccato beat of someone in the midst of a panic attack, but she wouldn't allow hysterical nerves to take control. She slowed her breathing.

Triste was covered to her chin in pale blue bed linens. Veya sat in the chair next to her and took her daughter's warm hand in her own. The many sounds in the room surprised Veya. Printouts were unspooling from several machines and the oxygen tubes connected to Triste's nostrils whirred along with the occasional ping of the heart monitor as it too unspooled its paper graphics of Triste's beating heart.

She squeezed her daughter's hand, praying to anything listening she'd feel a squeeze back. She held back tears and said, "Triste, sweetie. Can you hear me? Please wake up. Please?" When her daughter didn't move Veya smoothed strands of hair from her Triste's forehead and watched the back and forth movement of Triste's eyes under her closed lids. Triste's lips were held in a tight pout.

Veya recognized the all too familiar facial expression, having seen Triste's lips pinched in agitation many times during the screaming teenage years of slamming doors and emotional arguments. The expression always made an appearance when Triste knew she'd lost an argument to Veya's logical reasoning. Their most recent had been over Triste's desire to sit out the next term of college. She'd told Veya, "I don't fit in. I feel, well, I really don't know what I feel or want to do anymore. Nothing fits."

Veya had reassured her. "Everyone your age wonders if they're doing the right thing sweetie. You'll see. It'll work out." It had seemed such a huge issue to Veya then.

A nurse came to check the monitors. The tap of her fingers entering computer data accompanied the whir and ping of the machines.

She asked Veya before leaving, "Is there anyone I can contact for you? I can sit with her if you have phone calls to make."

"No, thank you." She couldn't say more for fear of the tears waiting to be released.

No one to call, there is no one. She'd made the decision so very long ago not to have her family in their lives. There had been only occasional phone calls to her sister in attempts to get her to visit. But she could never convince Brin to set foot off the Island.

Since she'd left the Island there'd been a single moment of weakness occurring a few weeks after Triste's birth. The baby had woken in the night with a high fever and started seizing the next day in the doctor's office. The doctor had stopped the seizure and afterward assured her, the cause had been the high fever, which lowered over the course of a few hours. The days following the incident she watched over Triste, and panicked at the baby's every move. She realized how alone they were in the world. So she'd written her mother announcing the birth of a granddaughter. Back then, there were no phones on the Island and mail was delivered weekly. She'd used a post office box as her return address, so her family wouldn't know the exact location of her home. She marveled now at her stupidity, as they hadn't once tried to find her in the three years since she'd left the Island.

A letter from her mother had arrived six weeks later.

So when are ya bringing her home to have the protection blessing done? She must receive her stone.

Mamma

At the time of the letter's arrival she'd been holding a giggling Triste, who had recovered from her illness. The thought of allowing the tiny infant to be wrapped in dead tree branches, and placed in the woods overnight, with nothing to protect her, and all for a worthless stone? She remembered startling her happy baby when she'd yelled, "No. Never."

Stones, everything in her mother's world revolved around them. Veya had ripped the leather strap that held her own stone from her neck the day after her grandmamma had died. Her grandmamma's beliefs were rooted in the rituals of Voodoo, not in those secretive ceremonies and beliefs revolving around stones held by her mother. Years after Veya left the Island, while talking on the phone with her sister Brin, her sister confided their grandmamma's sister was who'd passed on the closely held practices to Marie, their mother. She taught Marie how to become the Sorrow Keeper, the title given to her by the Islanders.

Veya had vowed her daughter would never know the cult her mother's people followed. She'd thrown the two-sentence letter her mother had written in the trash. When she heard a clink, she'd known a stone had fallen from the envelope. She'd immediately thrown the trash out.

The ping of the machines monitoring Triste's heart rate brought Veya back to present day. The nurse sitting outside the room signaled with the shake of her head there was no cause for alarm, and the day passed with more nurses coming in and out of the room checking the machines, taking notes. But her daughter never woke. By late afternoon, Veya felt she was suffocating. She needed fresh air. She told herself it would only be for a few moments. Once outside the building she found a bench.

The openness of the valley surrounding Ashland had drawn her to the area. She'd sought out an environment the exact opposite of the claustrophobic Island. On the Island she'd been surrounded by trees with branches always pulling at her hair, her clothes, and tripping her with their ever-crawling roots. Reluctantly, she had to admit, as a child, she'd never tired of the endless places to explore on the Island. A fantasyland for a kid, but as she grew, she realized in every shiny fantasy an ominous evil also lived.

Comforted by the wide-open view surrounding her, she allowed her mind to revisit the Island of her youth.

Arial maps of the Island showed a landmass of about eight miles long and six miles wide buried in Louisiana's southern Atchafalaya Basin. Parts of the land were under water at differing times of the year depending on rainfall. As money allowed, a teacher was hired for the Islanders' children, which meant some of the children never actually set foot off the piece of land, since the only way off was by a small flat-bottomed boat known by locals as a pirogue. The teachers, generally grad students, were lured by the possibility of studying the inhabitants' rumored ritualistic behaviors surrounding stones and their healing properties. However, they never stayed longer than their contracted time, after learning no off-lander would ever be allowed in the inner sanctum of a Sorrow Keeper's customs.

At the young age of twelve Veya had begun begging for employment at the only store on the Island, which was owned by her father. By the time she turned sixteen, she'd coaxed her way into being allowed to go with her father when he purchased supplies. This gave her the opportunity to travel off the Island frequently.

The Islanders lived simply. They used the store for supplies and had generators, a huge community garden, chickens, other small animals and the Gulf, rich with seafood. She knew her parents allowed her to work in the store with hopes of keeping her there. Their hopes were for naught.

She'd trained her sister, Brin, six years younger as best she could to take over for her when she left. Even at Brin's young age she caught on quite well, and Veya had every confidence she'd exceed Veya's abilities as their father's helper as she grew older. Brin, who'd eagerly taken to their mother's teachings and followed each and every ritual to perfection. Brin, who loved the Island and wore her stone proudly, often asking Veya why she did not. Veya's response was always the same. "I don't believe in any of Mamma's bayou superstitions."

By the time Veya shook off her ruminations of the Island she was startled to see the sun lowering in the sky over the valley. She stood and walked back toward the hospital. The blanket of misery tugged at her the closer she came to the building.

Halfway back she heard Triste's pleading voice coming from the hospital. "Mom, Mom, where are you, Mom? Help me, please. I can't find my way out. Help!"

She's awake!

Veya ran down the hallway toward the ICU. As the glass room came into view, realization dawned. She wouldn't have been able to hear Triste calling to her from so far away. The room was in a state of commotion. Dr. Ming leaned over Triste, listening to her heart. A nurse blocked Veya when she tried to enter the room.

"I'm her mother. What's wrong?"

Dr. Ming looked up and motioned for her to stay out. But within minutes he came out to speak to her. "I didn't want to alarm you when I spoke with you this morning, at least not until I had some type of explanation. I still don't have a diagnosis for the coma, or her heart rate dropping so low. This is the second time as it also occurred in the ER this morning. I know I should have informed you then, but as I said I'd hoped to have a diagnosis and treatment plan. But with it happening again … well, I felt it best you be told."

Veya tensed, and in a steady voice said, "You will not keep information from me, or I will have you removed as my daughter's physician. Is that understood?"

Dr. Ming looked from Veya to the room where Triste lay. "Yes, it is understood. May I say Dr. St. James you are looking not quite well yourself? You will do your daughter no good should you fall ill. I would suggest you go home and get some rest. As I have promised, I will let you know in the event of the slightest change."

Veya knew his recommendation for her to get some rest was what any doctor would tell her, but she would not leave Triste. She responded, her voice still laced with anger, "Right, you'll call me. Like you told me about her heart this morning? No, I'm staying. I'll let the nurses' station know which waiting room I'm in and I'll be checking in frequently until I'm allowed back beside my daughter."

A nurse appeared at her side and handed her a plastic sack. "These are your daughter's belongings."

Veya found an empty waiting room and opened the bag as soon as she sat down . Triste's purse lay on the top. Her insurance card was loose outside of her wallet. When Veya went to place it back she noticed a worn box of what she assumed to be playing cards sitting at the bottom of the purse. One of the cards had escaped the box. The image on it caught her attention. It wasn't an average playing card. She picked it up and immediately dropped it from her hand as though it were on fire.

A *Tarot card? Why would Triste have Tarot cards?* "Tellin' cards" is what Veya's grandmamma had called them. She retrieved the card and hid it back in the box, but the illustration on the card's front was seared in her brain—a body, male or female she couldn't tell, hung upside down from a tree limb by rope tied around the feet. The body appeared as if being pulled into a crack in the ground and through the roots of the tree. Partially buried in the soil and tree roots were skulls of varying sizes, both human and animal. The title written in bold black lettering above the image read, *The Hanged Man.* She shoved the box back in the purse. Her hand brushed against something soft. She pulled out a white velvet pouch that fit in the palm of her hand.

The nerve beside her right eye twitched when a memory of her mother's purple pouch flashed across her mind. With sweating hands, she opened the small bag.

If what was inside the bag had been a snake, heroin, or a supply of needles they wouldn't have scared her half as much as what she actually found. Stones. She counted out seven unevenly cut, taken from the earth and never turned or polished, crystalized stones. Amongst the stones were strands of moss.

The staccato beat of her heart came back full force. She leaned her head down between her knees, and took the deep breaths she'd been taught. Her heart slowly came back to its regular rhythm. The twitch around her eye remained.

How, how can Triste possibly have a pouch similar to Mamma's?

She threw the pouch into the purse and zipped it shut, not wanting to know anything else that might be revealed upon further inspection. When she went to put the purse back in the plastic bag the smell coming from inside the hospital bag stopped her. The overwhelming odor entered her nasal passages and her chest seized with pain, as though a sledgehammer had landed at its center. She carefully reached her hand inside the bag, and pulled out a nightgown, the same nightgown Triste had been wearing in her dream. With unsteady hands she caressed the embroidered roses on the collar of the gown. Mud and debris clung to the carefully stitched hem.

The cloth reeked of the smell she so desperately sought to escape—the Island.

Veya stopped at the nurses' station to make certain they had her cell number. Then she drove to Triste's apartment, running yellow lights while trying to escape the tightness of her chest. She had no time for panic. She had to get to Triste's home. She had questions for Mary. Where had Triste gotten those damn cards? Okay, the cards she could reason. Many people used them. But the stones ... *the stones, dear God in heaven, how did she get them?*

Chapter Three

Veya edged around the paving tiles Triste had insisted they create together despite Veya's protests and offer to pay for a smooth pathway to the apartment's entrance. How could she explain to her daughter the repulsion she'd experienced when placing each colored pebble in the cement mold? She rang the doorbell and knocked. When no answer came, she opened the door with the key Triste had given her in the event of an emergency. She'd tried phoning Mary before leaving the hospital, but had immediately been sent to voicemail. She assumed the woman had gone to stay with another friend.

She felt along the wall for the light switch and jumped when the light-filled room revealed hastily-moved furniture hugging the living room wall. She strode purposefully to her daughter's bedroom in order to escape the thought of paramedics carrying an unresponsive Triste out of the apartment.

The room's door stood open and showed a mess that her fastidious daughter would be embarrassed to have her mother see.

What am I doing here? What am I looking for? Out of habit, she started placing things back in order.

She put books on shelves, righted perfume bottles, and closed closet doors. But couldn't bring herself to remake the bed until she'd stripped it of the sheets Triste had been lying on, and replaced them. When she went to tuck the laundered sheets under the mattress, her hand nudged something hard—not between the mattress and box spring, but inside the mattress itself. She moved her hand over the area again and found nothing. But when she tucked in the overlapping bedspread her hand brushed against the object again, a thin square piece of cardboard sewn in the mattress covering. She tore the bed coverings off and searched the room for scissors.

Her mind immediately latched on to a *gris-gris* talisman her mother had placed in the seam of her pillow case when she was no more than five or six years old. She'd opened the pouch, and found a dried chicken foot. When she'd gone to throw the thing away, her mother had insisted she place it back saying, "Baby girl, it be a harmless protection from your dreams, and the creatures what come out only in the darkness."

With the memory fresh in her mind, Veya found scissors and placed them along the heavy seam of the mattress. But there proved to be no need, as the seam magically opened revealing Velcro had held it closed. Her hand snaked through the opening and pulled out a brown, soft leather book no larger than her hand. She'd never seen her daughter write in a journal.

The bed springs squeaked as she sat on its edge. She took a deep breath, and before opening the book whispered, "Triste, please forgive me for reading this. "

March 10th

Something is wrong with me. I hope writing down what's been happening, as Dr. Anderson pre-scribed, will help.

The date coincided with Triste's first therapy appointment. As Veya read the first entry, single words and phrases jumped off the page.

I had the dream again last night ... I'm in a forest ... There's a tree ... I hear my name called ... A big rat is chasing me ... It's pitch black ... I'm falling ...

What? Veya knew entire books had been written regarding falling dreams. Was it coincidence that in her own dream of her daughter the night before trees were behind Triste? She turned to the next page.

Interspersed with Triste's dreams were troubling entries about her spiraling depression. Veya yelled into the creeping darkness of her daughter's room, "Stupid. How deep did I bury my head in the sand not to have noticed how bad she'd gotten?" *Or has Triste gotten very good at hiding her true self from me?*

Veya scanned the next entry, over a month old. Again some words stood out while others faded to nothing.

September 1st

Yesterday Mary found a package … To Triste … a used deck of Tarot cards … a white pouch filled with colored stones … I asked Mary to do a reading on me … she turned over a card with the title Elder Wood … gnarled, intertwined trees … I screamed … I don't remember anything after. Am I going crazy? Who sent me such strange things?

Triste had drawn a rough sketch of the card on the next page.

Veya briefly toyed with the notion of her mother sending Triste the package. But other than to annoy Veya, she could not for the life of her come up with any reason why her mother would have cause, or reason, to do such a thing.

September 15th

I don't know how people live in this world with all its anguish and pain. How do they get out of bed? What's the point? I can't face Mamma. She'll be furious over my grades and the thought of seeing

Dr. Anderson makes me feel like I'd have to walk through quicksand to get there.

Veya turned to the last entry in the journal.

October 5ᵗʰ—Last Night

Mary and I really had it out. I asked her to move out two weeks ago. I can't take any more of her stalling and excuses. She says I need her here to look after me, but she's wrong. I'm so much calmer. I'm more at peace now that I know what I have to do. I have to stop fighting. I'll go where the voices want me to go. It's all so simple.

Voices? Oh, Triste!

Something drew Veya to turn the pages back to the first entry. The words she'd initially paid no mind to, or had she not wanted to see them? They now screamed at her … *a big rat is chasing me.* In the time it took the journal to fall to the floor her vision tunneled to a small dot. Her heart leapt from her chest to her throat. She leaned over, placed her head between her legs and slowed her breathing. *You will not pass out. You will calm down.* She repeated the mantra, over and over until her heart steadied, and her vision returned to normal. She retrieved the diary from the floor with shaking hands.

She read the entry over and over again before screaming in the deafening silence of her daughter's room, "An oversized rat, a swamp rat? What the hell?"

Veya's first panic attack had occurred while running from a swamp rat. She'd been ten years old, and running from the rodent when the overwhelming sensation of uncontrollable fear had hit her. A hypnotherapist unearthed the long-buried memory just days before Triste had been born. She'd never gone back to have her memory regressed again, but the session had served as the catalyst to ridding herself of the burdensome affliction of her panic attacks.

The therapist's notes had described the animal: Around four feet tall, with overly elongated fingers, thin spindly legs resembling tree twigs, and a tail as long as the animal was tall. Its ears were pointed, standing straight up from its skull; mud-brown skin hung in wrinkles off its bones.

Is that the rat Triste is seeing in her dreams?

Each word in the last entry of the diary was etched vividly on the inside of Veya's closed eyes. She couldn't escape her daughter's handwriting. *I'll go where the voices want me to go. It's all so simple.*

Veya was shaking with fear and confusion in the apartment where her daughter should've been. She jumped when her cell phone rang. She pulled it from her jacket pocket and almost dropped it when she saw it was her sister calling.

"Hello? Brin?"

"Veya, thank the Spirits you answered and didn't ignore my call. It's Mamma. She's slipped in ta a coma like Grandmamma did. I'm worried Veya. I need ya. Please come, and if'n Dr. Mary hasn't left yet, tell her we need her here, now. Please hurry. So many things have been happenin'. So many things I have ta tell ya."

Veya attempted to ask pointed questions, like "Who is Dr. Mary?" But Brin had begun sobbing, making her responses incoherent. So Veya ended the call telling her sister she'd call back within the hour.

Dr. Mary? Could Dr. Mary be the same Mary living with Triste?

Chapter Four

Veya sat motionless in her parked car outside of the hospital trying desperately to grasp on to any logical reasoning, something to make sense of her daughter's diary entries. She'd tried to erase from her mind what Triste had written. *I have to stop fighting it. I'll go where the voices want me to go.* Yet the words remained, and coupled with the phone call from Brin she was plunged back to the Island. Both her mother and Triste were in a coma.

A coincidence? They can't be tied. They can't!

Veya remembered the Island as a world filled with the delusional whisperings of a secretive underworld. A place where, at a very young age, she learned to lock away and never speak of those things she couldn't explain. As she got older, they became a kid's wild imaginings. Then as an adult, the Island became a place inhabited by people who suffered from a mental illness. A psychosis, which she had concluded, fed on their ritualistic practices and beliefs.

She pulled her phone from her purse, got out of her car and again tried Mary's cell. The voice box was full. "Dr.

Mary," her sister Brin had said. *If Mary is Brin's Dr. Mary, who the hell is this woman and how does she know Brin?*

Well, she'd soon find out. The hospital would have Mary's work schedule. She strode purposefully toward the entrance, and blinked when she saw Mary coming toward her as though she'd conjured her up through sheer will. Head down; the young woman's paces were so fast she resembled a speed walker verging on taking off into a full run. When she looked up and caught Veya's gaze, for a brief moment, Veya thought Mary would do just that. But Mary didn't run. She went right up to Veya.

"Veya, sorry I haven't returned your calls. I've had so many arrangements to make, but I swear to you, as soon as I got in the cab, I would've called you."

Veya wondered for a beat when she had become Veya to Mary, and not Dr. St. James. But the pained and unkempt look of Mary's appearance washed the thought aside. "What's wrong? Is it Triste?"

"No, well yes, and no. This does involve Triste, but … let's find an empty waiting area for privacy. I don't have much time."

"I really don't care about privacy. I want answers, *Dr.* Mary, is it? I thought you were a nurse? Brin told me to tell you they needed you back on the Island?" She waited to see the other woman's reaction. But Mary's face showed no surprise at Veya's question. "Who the hell are you?

What have you got to do with my family and what have you done to Triste? If you …"

Mary's condescending tone silenced Veya. "Please keep your voice down. Look, you can trust me or not. It's entirely up to you. Just know I had good reason for not revealing I'm both a clinical psychologist, and an RN. I maintained my RN license after beginning my private practice."

Through gritted teeth Veya asked again, "What do you have to do with my family?"

"Yes, I know your family. They called me to the Island two months ago."

"Called you to the Island? Why? Those people don't do *therapy*. More importantly why were you living with my daughter? I'll ask you one last time. What have you done to her?"

"I didn't *do* anything to your daughter. Your mother begged me to come here to help, to observe, to watch over Triste. It's a long, complicated story. I'm sorry I didn't realize. I didn't think this could happen—off Island." Her shoulders slumped and her tone shifted. She lowered her head. Her voice reached Veya in a whisper. "How, Marie? How could it have gotten to her so far away, and what am I to do now?"

"What did you say? Did you say Marie? Are you speaking about my mother, or do you actually think you're speaking to *her*? You have a psychic hot line? How long did you say you were there? Two months? You've spent two months on that godforsaken piece of dirt and you're already as off the rails as they are? Answer my question. What does this have to do with Triste?"

Mary looked directly at Veya, but said nothing.

Veya wanted to shake the woman, force her to speak. Instead she calmly asked, "You said, gotten to her. You mean Triste? What did someone do to Triste and who is it?"

Mary evaded Veya's direct question and instead said, "Triste is fine. Well, as fine as someone can be who is in a catatonic state."

"Catatonic?" Veya tried to recall the medical term, and how catatonic differed from coma.

Mary brushed the question aside. "Dr. Ming will have to be the one to explain."

"Fine, I'll talk to him about Triste, but you haven't answered my question. Why are you here and how is my family in any way tied to what is going on with my daughter?"

Mary sighed. "Your father contacted me. I live in Morgan City. I'm sure you remember it's where your father orders his store's supplies. I'd opened my practice there a few months before. I specialize in depression disorders and your father, worried about your mother's— as he called it—increasing melancholy, asked for my counsel. But after my first week on the Island, I realized her despair, and the Islanders increasing illnesses, went far beyond depression."

Mary seemed to want to stop her explanation there. Veya raised her left eyebrow while also narrowing her eyes to a slit. Mary continued. "I know you haven't visited the Island in years. At present, including the smaller strips of land surrounding it, there are roughly two hundred people living there. Over the last year, there've been thirty suicide attempts, twenty successful. Your father wanted answers, not only for the Islanders, but concerning your mother. When I left the Island her depression had lessened. I would never have left if I hadn't felt she would be okay. I'd been asking Brin to contact you. I'm glad she finally did."

"Has all this been some elaborate ploy to get me back to the Island? I will ask you only once more before I involve the police. What have you done to my daughter?"

Mary furrowed her brow in contemplation. "Marie Lyn St. James, your mother, is well … she's quite a unique individual, isn't she?"

"Stop right there. If you think I have some allegiance to my mother over my daughter you are sadly mistaken. I know my mother's mental state. I also know how everything is always about her. How she keeps everyone on the Island believing she is their queen or priestess or … fuck it. I cut off contact years ago. You scared of her? Well, if I find out you've done anything to my daughter, you'll have someone to truly fear."

Mary's eyes filled with tears and glistened in the harsh overhead lighting. "This is all so beyond my understanding. I've been in practice for less than a year." A nervous laugh bubbled from her before she continued. "Hell, I'm only a few years older than Triste. I've been so arrogant, so sure I could help them, help Marie and Triste. No, I'm not afraid of your mother. She's the one who sent me here. She somehow knew Triste suffered the same despondence she'd been experiencing. She wanted me to convince Triste, well, you and Triste, to go back to the Island."

Mary's nervous laughter increased. Her whole body shook while tears streamed down her face. Veya thought she was watching a mental breakdown right before her very eyes. When Mary finally calmed down, she looked up at Veya, her lips twisted in a sad grin. "I even thought I could help you."

For the beat of a second Veya felt sorry for her. "Yeah, well, many have tried. Hasn't anyone told you yet? We doctors make the worst patients. What did you mean when you said you didn't think it could happen off Island? You don't really believe Triste's depression has any connection to what's been occurring there, do you?"

"According to your mother, yes, because your daughter, is well, your daughter. Marie believes Triste is being pulled back to the Island to complete some ritual, which Marie will not explain to me. She believed if the ceremony wasn't completed Triste would slip into this catatonic state, or worse. She believed Triste could die. It appears she was right."

"What the …" Fear tore at the edges of the leaden apron of weight surrounding Veya's body, but could not penetrate it. "No, no, I don't believe it. What did you do to my daughter? Does she know about any of this nonsense?"

"I did nothing to Triste, other than to try to get her to go to her appointments with Dr. Anderson. I know I should've spoken to you sooner. I've told you all I know. Now, I have to go. Dr. Anderson is waiting for me. He's agreed to assist with the Islanders."

"Dr. Anderson? My associate? Triste's therapist? What? Why didn't either of you tell me any of this before now?"

"Patient client confidentiality, Dr. St. James. You understand. Neither your father, or mother, nor Triste, would allow Dr. Anderson, or myself to confide in you. But now your mother can't give consent, so your father has, and with Triste in danger, I have no choice. Again, according to your mother, you are Triste's only hope of surviving. I'm sorry but I really do have to go."

Veya stood in the doorway blocking Mary's departure. "No, not without answers. Have you read my daughter's diary? Did you give her the stones, the cards?"

"I'm sorry. I truly am, but I need answers too and the only place I can get them is down there. Your mother and

I, over the weeks I cared for her, we became very close. I promised her so many things. Now I have to get back to her and like it or not, so do you. I believe her, Veya. I know none of this makes any rational sense. But the medical diagnoses aren't giving us any answers either, are they?" Mary pushed Veya aside and walked toward the hospital exit.

Veya fought the urge to go after her, but then Mary turned and said, "You should know, those ten people who attempted suicide, but weren't successful—we're not sure their families are telling us the truth. You know how superstitious the Islanders can be. Veya, those ten people, each and every one of them is in the same catatonic state as Triste and your mother."

"What? Dr. Ming must be told about this. It's you, you've brought something, some kind of virus with you from the Island and transferred it to Triste." Relief held Veya's fear at bay. Finally, something concrete to follow-up on. A virus buried in the muck of the swamp could even explain her grandmamma.

Mary shook her head and said, "Oh, if only it were that easy. I've spoken to Dr. Ming and he's since been in contact with the physicians taking care of the Islanders. He's confirmed they've run every test he has or will prescribe for Triste. There is no bug, no strain of virus, no medical disease for her catatonic state."

"But there has to be." Veya grasped for reason.

Mary tried one last time to sway Veya. "Without Marie, how will we ever find a way to help her or Triste? You and Triste were her only concern. She wanted you both back on the Island where she could protect you. You really want to help your daughter, Dr. St. James? You know where you have to go. You've known all along. Marie said to tell you to bring the cards and the stones, and not to forget your own protection stone." Mary caressed the necklace Veya had seen her fingering when she'd first arrived at the hospital. She now realized why she noticed the stone in the first place, because of its rough-cut and unpolished setting.

She watched Mary exit the hospital then turned and walked toward Triste's room, her mind refocused on what Mary had said. *Catatonic?* She intended to check in at the nurses' station to see if she could speak privately with Dr. Ming, but as a nurse came into sight he called her, requesting she stop by his office before going in to see Triste.

Upon entering his office, she counseled herself. *Triste is fine. Catatonic? Is it a worse diagnosis than coma? Don't borrow sorrow.* As soon as the phrase entered her mind, the rose scented powder her grandmamma always patted on her face each morning surrounded her and she heard her saying, "Don't borrow sorrow, child, there be more than enough of it to come ta ya all on its own."

Sitting across from Dr. Ming she braced herself for whatever he had to report. "I spoke with Mary on the way in. She said Triste is catatonic?"

"Yes, there has been some activity. Triste opened her eyes, and at first I thought she'd indeed awoken."

Veya's heart pulsed. "She's awake?"

Dr. Ming raised his hand. A motion she assumed he'd used many times when trying to get patients' families to stop talking and listen. "Please let me explain. Catatonic patients will do this. They seem to be awake. They can go in and out of this state for quite some time. But they aren't awake, they're not conscious of their actions. While I'm pleased she's not in a coma, I'm still quite concerned."

Veya opened her mouth to speak, and again received the hand motion.

"Yes, there has been a change in your daughter's diagnosis from coma to catatonic. Please know I called you as soon as I could. My immediate concern was to assess and stabilize your daughter. After she appeared to wake up, she never spoke, but did move her hand and foot as I instructed. All of this occurred in a matter of seconds, she then became quite agitated and experienced another incident with her heart. We used the defibrillator again to get its rhythm back to normal. We're monitoring her very closely, but I still haven't discovered the cause of her heart irregularity, or her catatonic state. The toxicology reports came back and revealed nothing to indicate a substance causing Triste's sudden condition. I believe Nurse Doucette, Mary, informed you I specialize in cases such as these? I've requested the files of the patients she alerted me to on the secluded island in Louisiana."

Damn, why didn't I ask Triste her new roommate's full name? Maybe the familiar southern surname of Doucette would've had me pushing Mary for answers sooner.

"Mary said you had a specialty. I understood your specialty to be coma cases not easily explained by a head trauma?"

"Let me answer your question by saying I've seen this type of catatonic behavior in chronically depressed individuals. Those patients are my specialty. In the cases I've studied, the patients had gone years in and out of depression, and most had several prior suicide attempts despite their treatment."

"And the outcome?" Veya said the words slowly, fearful of his response.

"I've had some success with electro-shock therapies. But those that do wake require intensive therapy and medication for the remainder of their lives. The rest remain catatonic for years and older studies report they eventually die of natural causes, never waking. My concern for your daughter is the catatonic behavior, coupled with her heart irregularities. I wish I could give you answers, but there simply are none at this time."

Dr. Ming had stopped talking. Veya knew he waited for more questions. But for the first time since Triste had been admitted, she had none.

Veya left the office intending to go sit beside Triste, but instead she found an empty family room. She needed time to think, to clear her head. She should call Brin back. *Poor sweet Brin, how worried she must be.*

Veya laid her head back against the well-worn sofa. Her eyelids closed. *It's impossible. There's no way Triste can be connected to the Island. There has to be something else, some other explanation.*

Veya couldn't untie the knot twisting in the pit of her stomach. A gust of heat settled around her along with the stench of stagnant water. The knot twisted tighter. She cautiously opened her eyes. Triste stood in the doorway of the small waiting room dressed in the same nightgown she'd been in when she appeared at the foot of Veya's bed. The nightgown, no longer white, was caked in mud. The embroidered flowers looked as though a seam ripper had been taken to them. A huge tree loomed behind Triste. Her long auburn hair clung in jagged, wet strips to the sides of her face. Veya moved toward her daughter, her hand reaching to see if the apparition before her was real. The tips of their fingers momentarily touched, before a tree branch wrapped around Triste's waist. An instant later the tree's massive trunk split open; a cavernous hollow. Triste was jerked through the opening. Veya once again watched helpless, as her daughter dissolved through murky darkness. The tips of her fingers, where they'd touched Triste's, were wet. She looked away for a moment and when she looked back the doorway was empty. Though the apparition had made no sound, Veya knew she'd never be able to erase the vision of her daughter's mouth open in a voiceless scream.

She spent the next few hours sitting by Triste's bedside watching in awe when Triste opened her eyes and obeyed when Veya asked her to squeeze her hand. Triste, the only person alive who could make Veya laugh till her sides ached; Triste, her only reason for waking many mornings. Veya needed to see awareness beaming from her daughter's open eyes. She needed to hear her laugh, cry—anything other than the unaware shell lying in the hospital bed.

Veya knew what she had to do, where she had to go. The answers, if there were any, were on the Island.

She called her sister. She hadn't spoken to Brin in over six months. She should've known something was wrong as Brin had been calling Veya more frequently, giving her hope that Brin might one day visit her in Ashland. Their conversation was brief, filled with Brin's pleas for Veya to come home.

Finally understanding she had no choice but to go back to the Island, Veya searched her address book for someone she could rely on to check in on Triste. When she'd first entered the hospital, she had little trust in the institution, and now she had even less. Veya had left no time in her life for friends so in the end Daniel was the person she called. She couldn't reasonably understand why, but she somehow knew he'd remain by Triste's side if she asked him to. Tears flowed freely down her face when he readily agreed.

The drive to the airport gave her many opportunities to turn around. But in the end her fears for Triste overshadowed her dread of returning to the Island.

At the airport Veya pulled her wallet out and handed her credit card to the smiling, too perky young woman behind the airline counter. When she went to return her wallet she noted the pouch she'd taken from Triste's apartment was still in her purse along with the cards.

As she sat waiting for the plane to board, she pulled the small bag from her purse. Her mother's words relayed by Mary came to her, "Bring your own protection stone." She pictured the stone buried by years of mud and sediment in the swamp where she'd flung it hanging from its rawhide string the day after her grandmamma had died. For a fleeting moment concern for its loss, and its perceived purpose gripped her. She loosened the superstition's hold with reason. *Why do I care? I don't believe in protection stones.*

She pulled out the box of cards—telling cards—and went to set them aside, but a string caught in its lid left the box half open. She pulled it loose; a circular, brown leather cord. The air in her lungs evaporated. *It can't be.* No stone dangled from its circle, but she could clearly see the well-worn notch where something had once hung. And like a phantom limb long ago severed, she once again felt the bulging tied off knot at its end biting into the skin at the nape of her neck. As a child she'd been forced to wear a lanyard identical to the one she held. At age nine she'd torn the cord from her body and fed it and the stone to the swampy marsh of the Island. Scratching the back of her neck as though the thing still lay there burrowing into her skin, she reached for the pouch and poured the stones out of the sack. Air returned to her lungs when she didn't see the stone given to her at birth amongst them. *How? This can't be the same piece of leather.*

The airport intercom announced the boarding of her flight.

She closed her eyes and visualized her place of serenity, the bench in the park. But instead of the park, the apparition of Triste in a voiceless scream appeared.

The heavy weight that had followed her from the hospital tightened. Along with it the thought of going back to the Island caused a whole new kind of terror to ripple through her. The narrow tunnel leading to the plane reminded her of the hallways of the hospital. She'd much rather have been there, encased in its sterile smells and stark white walls, than where she was going. The mist shrouded world of the Island loomed large in her mind.

Chapter Five

Waves of heat undulated off the murky water surrounding the wharf where Veya stood. Her clothes clung damp against her skin. She noted the time on her watch, five p.m. Back in Ashland the day would be cooling down, but she wasn't in Ashland. A sun-shriveled, toothless man sat on the edge of the wharf wiping sweat from his face with a red handkerchief while his secured pirogue floated idly below him. She breathed a sigh of relief when she did not recognize him. Her sister had acquiesced to her request and hired a complete stranger to take her out to the Island. At least she assumed him to be here for her, since they were the only two people occupying the weatherworn walkway.

He stood as she moved toward him, extended his hand to take her duffle bag and said, "You be Miss Veya? Why, you done grown and gots a child of your own I hear? I be Alcee. I don't suppose you be rememberin' me? I used to do some deliverin' out to your daddy's store?"

"Yes, I'm Veya and sorry, no, I don't remember you." They were the only words she could manage through the emotion of being back, back to this place she had promised herself she'd never see again. Thankfully he wasn't a non-stop talker the way she'd remembered most Cajun men were. He carefully placed her bag in the middle of his pirogue, and held the boat steady as she stepped down and sat on a sagging wooden slat at the boat's center.

His only other words to her were, "Sorry ta hear 'bout Tante Marie. My family, we be keepin' candles lit and rosaries goin' ever since the news hit land."

She thanked him, knowing her mother was in no way his aunt, or any relation for that matter. Any land-walker who paddled or motor-boated the five or more miles to the Island seeking her mother's counsel called her "Tante Marie."

Alcee cranked the motor and the boat skipped along, water spewing from its back until they reached the dense masses of land Veya had seen a good mile away from the wharf. Once they got close to the marshy masses, Alcee cut the motor and began paddling.

The sweat clinging to her body turned to a bone deep chill when they entered one of the many densely overhung, narrow fingers of the swamp. The sun swiftly disappeared behind the low hanging charcoal gray clouds covering the center area where she knew the Island stood surrounded by many smaller strips of land. The boat made a sharp turn down another narrow byway, cutting through the dense green carpet of water lilies floating upon the inky water.

The deeper they traveled through the wetlands, the more her head filled with memories. Alcee turned to her, but instead of his face, she'd flashed back to childhood, and her father's grinning face stared back at her. A pile of sacks filled with flour, sugar, bottles of thick cane syrup and the smell of ground coffee surrounded them both. His jovial voice was weaving one of his many stories about his own mamma; the tale where she'd pulled a hunk of sugarcane hanging from her mouth, like a cigar, half chewed, offering him his very first bite of the sweet stalk.

Another memory hit her. The image of Brin's red-pinched, innocent, trusting face staring up at Veya minutes after her birth. The memories came at her in waves, and were so thick she actually batted at the air around her head in an effort to make them stop. When Alcee turned a questioning eye she said, "Bugs."

He grinned in agreement.

She returned to her own thoughts, thoughts of how she'd grown, matured beyond the anger, the fears, the confusion of her childhood. She'd laid on many a proverbial therapist's couch, sat in every manner of group therapy chair, and contorted her body crossed-legged on ancient rugs in deep meditation. All in an attempt to exorcise the demons she now hoped she'd truly outrun. But the closer they got to the Island the harder her heart pounded and the more cold sweat dripped from her body. The familiar tightening in her chest spread through her like a cancer. With each deep breath she inhaled in an attempt to rid her body of the menacing anxiety, wafts of the dead buried things decomposing beneath muddy water entered. Finally, she closed her eyes, and conjured the face of a smiling Triste. But even Triste's face couldn't replace the mass of land fast approaching.

The Island.

A flash of Brin's red hair peaked from the foliage surrounding the Island's edge. Her sister's auburn head disappeared as the boat slowly floated up to the weathered pilings holding the wharf above the stagnant water of the bayou. Swirls of evening fog crawled along the water's dark, syrupy surface. Veya wrapped her arms protectively around her body. The bland sandwich she'd eaten on the plane threatened to make a reappearance. Alcee tied the boat and offered his hand to help her up and onto the wharf. She looked toward the Island. Twisted tree roots lined its bank giving the impression the land wasn't soil, but a floating mass of gnarled, bark-covered snake-like creatures long ago buried in an ancient nest.

What am I doing here?

When she looked from the Island to the wharf, she expected to see Alcee's hand extended to hers. Instead it was Brin's. She helped Veya from the boat and onto the wharf. Her sister, no longer a girl, but a grown woman, wore a bright yellow, ankle length, cotton skirt and a white, peasant-style short-sleeved blouse. She could've been Triste's twin sister with her tiny frame of just an inch over five feet and flowing red hair. Veya saw sadness and a flash of unease behind her sister's forced smile before Brin said in a slow southern drawl, "Welcome, home, Veya. It been way too long, sha."

Veya, overwhelmed with both emotion and dread managed to say, "Please take me to Mamma."

She followed Brin as though in a dream. By the time her mind began to clear they were walking toward the mound of tree roots.

Did one of the roots slither toward the water?

They continued to walk along a dirt-packed trail toward town, or as Veya thought of it, *the village*. To fill the time she told Brin unimportant details of her life in Ashland. Brin in turn spoke of changes in the Island inhabitants Veya might remember; there were a few weddings and births, but mainly deaths and illnesses. Each carefully avoided talking about their mother or Triste. She thought of asking Brin if she currently had anyone special in her life. Her sister had been in two serious relationships that she knew of, but each had ended, and she'd never married. *The clock is ticking, little sister.* But she didn't ask. It took every ounce of energy she could channel not to run to the wharf and scream for Alcee to take her back. Her mind wove just such a scenario when the toe of her shoe caught on something. If not for Brin catching her, she would've gone down, face first.

"Damn. What the …" She looked back to see what had tripped her and then back up toward where they were going. Tree roots, identical yet smaller than those she'd seen along the Island's muddy banks, laced along the entire path.

Without her having to ask, Brin answered the question forming in Veya's mind. "Been this way for some time now. Just keeps growin' more. Ever' time I come out here there be more roots on the path. Caused some damage in town. Well, you'll see."

By the time they entered the town dusk had fallen, wrapping all the buildings in shadows. An occasional small patch of colored paint showed through a lighted window or reflected off a porch light. The town consisted of a single street lined by about a dozen homes with their father's store at the center. Trees and undergrowth surrounded it on all sides. A church stood at the end of the dead-end street. Its spire cast a shadowed cross on the dirt-packed road from the full moon rising behind it.

Brin hadn't been entirely forthcoming with her description of the tree roots' damage. Even in the darkness Veya could see empty shells of at least two homes that had roots growing out of their glassless windows. The homes that had been spared had root-barked walls surrounding them, making them appear ready for battle against some unknown danger. Past the town a quarter mile the house

Veya had vowed she'd never set eyes on again, waited for her return.

When the home came into view, she tried in vain to catch her muffled alarm. A strangled squeal escaped her. Tree roots surrounded it, like those in town. But those surrounding her family's home were much larger, coming from the dense woods that stood watch behind the house. The roots were thickest at the back of the home rising as tall as the single-story structure with its eight-foot ceilings and an attic you could stand in. They came from the back, circling on either side and narrowing in circumference to about a foot before splintering off in several fingers of roots at the very front of the home where she stood trying to fathom what her eyes were seeing.

Brin moved to go past her, but Veya reached to stop her. She had questions. Why hadn't she asked them before now? Her sister shook her hand off and stepped over the smaller roots, climbing the two steps to the screened-in front porch and disappearing through the open door.

Veya tried to take in the reality of the home encased by enormous tree roots. When she looked toward the open doorway her father stood framed by the porch light.

His once coal black hair was now peppered with white. Wiry strands standing straight up in places gave him the appearance of a mad man. His six foot four frame was stooped and bent as though he should've been leaning on a walking stick to keep him balanced. Exhaustion weighed in his voice and showed in his blue eyes as he said, "Well ya finally come home, did ya? I told her ya would."

Veya walked to him, and tensed at his one-arm, awkward hug.

He led her silently down the long hallway past her childhood bedroom, then past Brin's and stopped. Pointing toward the last room's open door he said, "Your mamma been waitin' on ya. I'll be in the kitchen when ya be done." He turned and left her standing alone.

She hesitated in the doorway, then stepped inside. Brin leaned over their mother, whispering, but stood when Veya entered and said, "I'll leave you two alone. When you done here, you and me got ta make plans 'bout tomorrow. I know you got questions. I hope I got answers."

Veya stood over her mother and recognized the striking resemblance she shared with the woman who'd birthed her. Had Veya not bleached her hair blond they could've passed as sisters as opposed to mother and daughter. From her mother's waist length black hair and sharp cheekbones to her six-foot frame, she'd inherited every physical trait. Veya noted her mother's nightgown open at the neck and the absence of the garnet stone that had eternally rested there. She briefly contemplated why it was missing, but her thoughts soon overcame her curiosity and locked on to the many things she'd wanted to say to the motionless woman. How many times had she played out telling her mother, "You failed me. The secrets you kept followed me my whole life. They almost destroyed me."

Veya turned to leave the room, but Marie's hand lifted, reaching out for her, an involuntary spasm. For a moment Veya pitied the woman whose unseeing eyes stared at the ceiling. But the movement reminded her of Triste's own phantom flailings, and the pity left, replaced by her familiar anger toward a vibrant, all knowing Marie. The woman who, on the day Veya had left the Island, had not gone to the wharf to tell her eighteen-year-old daughter, good luck, or I love you, or please don't go. The woman who she knew, in some way, was to blame for Triste's illness.

Comforted by her anger and thinking of Triste lying alone in the hospital, she leaned to whisper in her mother's ear. "The one time you could help me and you're not here again, Mother. I know you had something to do with whatever is going on with Triste. I'm going to stop you, get my daughter back, and never set foot in this house again."

She left the room with Marie's hand still reaching out toward her.

She dropped her bag in her old bedroom and went in search of her father, hoping he'd have answers to her questions. When she entered the kitchen, the smell of the chicken and sausage gumbo boiling on the stove gave her a brief moment of comfort. Her father sat with his back to her, bent over the pale green Formica kitchen table where she'd eaten countless meals. In front of him were her mother's Tarot Cards spread out in a half circle. *If hers are here, where did the pack I found in Triste's apartment come from?*

He held a solitary card in his hand. She'd never seen her father with the cards before. A new fear squeezed its way through her already crowded brain. *He's lost it. She's in a coma and his mind's gone.*

"Dad?"

When he turned to her, instead of the crazed eyes she'd anticipated, a profound sadness reflected back through their blue irises. He held up the card in his hand and said, "Ya remember how your grandmamma used the cards? She didn't take no store in the normal ways of using 'em. She called 'em tellin' cards, and said ya need only pull one ta see what need told. I thought I'd see what they be tellin' today. This bein' a special day, when both my daughters be under my roof again." He showed her the card in his hand. "This here is what come up. It says, *Judgment.* What ya think it be tryin' ta say, this headless woman with a child on either side a' her? Is it fore-tellin' your mamma's not in her head no more? Then, where is she? I gots ta believe this be the right card tryin' ta tell me somethin', cause there be two girls standin' on either side a this here headless woman."

Succumbing to hunger Veya pulled a bowl from a cabinet, and placed white rice in it before filling the bowl to the brim with gumbo. She then sat next to her father. Between bites she said, "Dad, you know I don't believe in any of this." She waved a hand over the cards. "What can *you* tell me? What's going on here?"

Still holding tightly to the card, he continued as though he hadn't heard her, "You know I been thinkin' on what I was goin' ta say to ya. I'm sorry for how we left things. Sorry for not trying ta see ya or your baby girl. But your mamma, well, she needed me and Brin needed me. And time passes so fast, don't it?"

Her mother needed him. The concern she'd been feeling for him left. It had always been about what her mother wanted. She took a deep breath before saying, "Yes, time passes and Mamma always gets what she wants, right, Daddy? And now my daughter is somehow mixed up in Mamma's craziness. So again, what can you tell me about what's going on?"

He laid the card down face up on the table and wiped at his eyes. "You know I got no knowin' on your mamma's ways. Never wanted ta know, never asked. I figure she ain't doing no harm. Hell, seems to me she done lots a good. Takin' away people's sufferin' the way she's done. Now look where it got her. Now she be the one sufferin'."

Veya's raised voice echoed in the small room, "Seriously? You really expect me to believe you have no knowledge of what …"

Before her eyes her father turned from the sympathetic man who'd raised her to the reserved stoic man he'd been when she left. He cut her off and said, "The way I see she done good, and she brought lots a money to the Island with all the land walkers who come here. You ain't never been interested in our lives, always lookin' for a way off the Island. So don't be comin' in my house and passin' judgment on her, or me." He picked up the card, looked closely at it and then laid the card back down before getting up and leaving her alone in the kitchen. She stared at its upturned face with the single word in bold black letters at its heading—*Judgment.*

She placed her empty bowl in the dishwasher, left the kitchen and went in search of Brin. She found her on the front porch, in their mother's old bentwood rocking chair. Veya sat in its twin next to her sister and said, "What's going on, and what can it possibly have to do with me and my daughter?"

"I been tryin' ta piece things out in my mind. Near as I can figure Mamma went out to the tree to talk to the Mortlins 'bout Triste. She had Triste's stone with her when she left the house. I seen the stone round her neck and asked her why she be havin' two stones. She said she been a keepin' Triste's stone safe till the time she be givin' it to her. I never knew she been holdin' it for Triste 'afore then. First time I'd ever laid eyes on it."

The pendant Veya's grandmamma had given her warmed against her skin, giving her comfort. She stood and paced the porch. Tightness constricted in her chest—lingering anger, not the debilitating anxiety. "Triste doesn't have a damn stone. Why would she? She's never been here, was never taken to the tree at birth; none of this, none of this insane superstition has anything to do with her."

Brin continued as though Veya had not spoken a word. "I found Mamma at the base a' the tree. I thought she be dead for sure, with her skin caked in dried blood, her hair all tangled with twigs and such, and her dress torn like somethin' had taken a sharp scissors to it. But when we got her home there weren't a mark on her. Does your educated brain got a reasonin' for that?"

Brin's methodical rocking and monotone voice made Veya want to run screaming from the house. Instead she held the rocker where her sister sat steady and in a raised voice said, "This is crazy. You know it's all Mamma's strange, conjuring bullshit. Some nut-bag off-lander probably didn't get what they wanted and attacked her. Where's this stone that's supposedly Triste's?" Brin pulled loose from Veya's grip and continued rocking.

"Mamma didn't have her stone, or any stone when I found her. They was both gone. Did I tell ya there be two

Mortlin' creatures there with her? First time I ever laid eyes on one up close. I think they the reason why she still be breathin'."

"Mortlings? What the hell are those, more superstitious nonsense? How do you know you weren't just seeing things? I mean if Mamma was as messed up as you say, they were probably just swamp rats who attacked her."

Brin sighed. "Don't be foolish, Veya. Mamma be the Mortlins' Keeper. I be knowin' what a swamp rat looks like. There be somethin' not right, but that ain't it."

"Fine. Then why didn't you try to talk to them to see what happened? Aren't you like Mamma? Don't they talk to you? Yeah, why didn't you talk to the monsters in the tree? I'm sure they have all the answers."

Brin has lost it just like our mother.

When her mother had told Veya of her "mind talkin'" to mythical creatures the absurdity of it had been all Veya needed to convince herself of her mother's unstable mental state. She'd tried to sway her father. Tried to get him to take her mother to the mainland and have a doctor examine her, talk to her. But Veya's distrust of her mother caused a rift between them. A chasm they'd never repaired. A few weeks after, she'd left the Island and never returned.

Veya looked out of the screened porch at the giant tree roots—something out of a Grimm's fairytale. Brin, who had stopped rocking, stood and walked behind her, placing her hand on Veya's shoulder.

Without turning, Veya said, "You have to understand. I may have seen one of those things you say were laying next to our mother once. A swamp rat, nothing more. It's taken years of therapy to have the thing stop chasing me in my dreams."

Brin said in a hushed whisper, "They was dead. The two I found with Mamma be dead, and since Mamma's been asleep I ain't seen any. It's one a' the things I been tryin' ta piece. I think all a' them, they all gone back down in the tree, and I'm a'thinkin' they took your Triste with 'em."

Veya turned to face her sister. "Took? Took? Triste is in a hospital in Ashland, Oregon. Can you please make sense?"

Brin turned from her sister, motioning for her to stay on the porch, and went inside the house. When she came back out Veya sat rocking. Brin handed her a large book that barely fit on her lap. Its worn leather binding and page edges were so yellowed Veya thought they'd disintegrate if touched.

"Mamma said if ya ever come here askin' 'bout things I was to give ya this. The book be writings explainin' 'bout the beginnin' a' things. She said ya never wanted to know, but if'n ya asked, I could give ya this." When Veya lifted the book it seemed to pulse in her hand. She dropped the tome back in her lap and reached for the comfort of her grandmamma's overly warm pendant,

She started to ask the hundred questions floating in her brain, but Brin gently placed her hand over Veya's mouth to stop her.

"Tomorrow's goin' ta be a tryin' day on both a' us, so if'n I be you I'd be gettin' some rest after your readin'."

"Why, what are we doing tomorrow?"

"Tomorrow we be goin' out to the Tree and if'n it'll let us—well—I'm still piecin' those things together." Brin hesitated in the doorway of the house and said, "Don't go wanderin' outside 'cause the night is when the roots do they growin'. So if'n ya hear a kind a suckin', slitherin' noise, that be all it is, roots a growin'. Night, Veya, hope your sleep is restful."

Sucking tree roots? Come on. Keep your mind on reality and try to make sense of this insanity so you can help Triste.

Chapter Six

Veya sat surrounded by night. The vibrant full moon shining above the canopy of trees covering her childhood home could not penetrate the dark. The porch lamp shone like a spotlight onto the worn, brown leather journal resting in her lap. Mosquitos hit against the screened-in front porch, and despite a slight breeze the oppressive heat was suffocating. She pulled at the neck of her damp T-shirt, but found no relief from the brief motion. With an image of Triste lying motionless in the hospital bed held in her mind, she opened the book and began reading.

Bertha June St. James—1840

I be the first ever Keeper ta have the gift a writing. This here be my accounting on the beginning a' things. It be passed from one Keeper ta the next till it be told ta me. There be only one Keeper at a time. When the signs be right, she be chosen and given teachings on the ways of a Keeper. The final teachings is told only in the time when the old Keeper is starting ta breathe they last.

But this here recording ain't bout all the Keepers who done come 'afore me. It be bout the Being what begun us as its Keeper. The Being and the Tree it and its kin be birthed from, the Tree where they lived long 'afore humans walked this land.

In the beginning there be one Being with four legs, four arms and two heads all coming from out a one chest. It be like the Maker of All had but one body ta sew two Beings on to. All the Being knew was the world inside a' the Tree, an eternally dark and woeful place, a home dug out a bark, and rock. It be a web a many paths with water flowing beneath it where other trees growed upside down like they be trying ta escape the roots a the Tree what birthed them and the Being. In this time, the Being never left the Tree.

Then The Maker of All shook the earth and the Tree split open and the Being seen there was another world outside a the Tree. The Being also seen its halves be different. One side be black like the eternal darkness of its home and the eyes in its head was red. The other side was green like the things growing outside a' the Tree and its eyes was a white light like the round ball up in the sky. The sun.

The green half wanted to escape the Tree, but the black half clung ta the roots growing in the Tree, making its other half stay. The first time the green half was able ta pull its other half out a' the Tree, the ball in the sky was shining. The green half picked up a rock of a color it had never seen, before its other half dragged it back down in ta the Tree. During this time, they was always pulling at each other. The green half wanting ta leave the Tree, the other half wanting to stay. Finally, the time come when each half had clawed at the other till they be ripped apart where they was joined. The Maker of All healed them. Then they was two Beings.

The green half what went outside a' the Tree be the ones we be Keepers of, cause we gots our ways a keepin' 'em safe. They got no sounds, no words, no mouths for talking. They got a kind a whisperin' comes to a Keeper, not in her ears, but in her head telling her things.

In the beginning they be called Stone Collectors, cause they begun collecting stones when they left they Tree underworld, and they other half. In the beginning the stones was they way a' tryin' ta get they other half ta go out a' the Tree. When they went down ta see 'bout they other half they buried the stones in the roots growing inside the Tree, hoping they other half would follow the stones out *a' the Tree. Over time a knowin' come ta the Stone Collectors that there be another reasoning ta why they was collecting stones and bringing 'em to they other half, and to the Tree. But they had no true reasoning on what the stones was a'doing or why they could still feel they other half, even when they weren't with 'em.*

In this time they other half, be called Light Stealers. They never left they Tree. You be seeing how they come by they name later in this here accounting.

For many a'earth cycles the Stone Collectors be the only two-legged walkers outside a' the Tree. Then the time come when The Maker of All put other two-legged walkers on the land—Humans.

The Stone Collectors studied the Humans' ways, but hid from 'em fearing they'd kill 'em for food. During this time, they kept taking stones down in ta the Tree to show they other half. But in the dark of they underworld they kin couldn't see the true colors a' the stones. They tried ta tell the Light Stealers in they mind whisper talking 'bout the different colors and 'bout the Humans. But they other half didn't want to know anything about the other walkers. They wanted only to stay in they underworld, and they wanted they other half to stay with 'em.

Then the time come when The Stone Collectors stopped comin ta see bout they other half and the Light Stealers went deeper down in ta the Tree. In this time the Light Stealers come to hate any light, and blamed the stones, and the Humans for taking they other half away from 'em.

That be when the warring time come.

Durin' the warring time, the Light Stealers come out from they underworld in the blanket of night, when no moon was shining. They stole they other half, and forced 'em down in ta the Tree underworld. Many died. There also be tales of Humans being stolen and never seen again. In this time, the Stealers begun to whisper dark thoughts in ta the Humans' minds, and no light shined on the land. Gray clouds covered they world. This be how the Light Stealers come ta get they name, cause they stole the light from they other half and the Island.

This be the time when we Keepers come ta being.

The first Human ta see a Stone Collector or Light Stealer and live ta tell 'bout it was a St. James woman. She was a grieving the death of her first-born girl child and had gone in the woods in search a' the Tree. Her people feared the Tree 'cause a' the tales of creatures from another world living in it and taking people. The woman had no fear a dying; she was a courtin' it.

She come upon the Tree. On one a' its gnarled roots a Stone Collector was being dragged by a Light Stealer. That be the first time a Stone Collector whispered in a St. James woman's mind asking her ta help it. It said, "I'm dying."

Its small size reminded her of the child she'd just lost so she fought with the Light Stealer ta keep it from taking the Stone Collector, and her very self, in ta an opening in the Tree. In the end, she killed the Light Stealer with a stone from a pile the Stone Collector had been a gathering.

When she seen the Stone Collector was truly dying, she gathered the pile a stones and put them on its body. Then she sat next ta the being, while words flowed from her mouth. The being sat up, and was healed.

Veya read less faded words written in the margin: *At some point in our history we learned the beings' true names. Stone Collectors are "Mortlings" and Light Stealers are "Hadlings."*

Veya let the book fall into her lap and shifted in the rocking chair. *Two creatures?* She'd been questioning whether she could accept the reality of one, how could she grasp, much less believe, in two, or any of what she was reading. *Keep reading Veya, remember this is for Triste.* She continued.

The St. James woman become the first Keeper.

The light come back to the land, and the Light Stealers went back down in ta they Tree. Even in the shelter of night with no moon they never come back out. The St. James woman had worked her teachings so the Light Stealers could never have power over they other half again. Some a' her teachings be known today as Voodoo. The other teachings, the ones she used ta heal the Stone Collector be known only to a Keeper, and be told ta the Keeper through the mind whispering of the Stone Collectors.

This be the time when we come to be Keepers.

The first Keeper, still grievin' her dead child, come to a knowing, if she give a Stone Collector a stone, her sorrow would be taken from her. Over time, other folks be told 'bout St. James women, and they stone juju. So they bring they sorrow and stones ta the Island and they leave with they grief lifted. That be how we be called Keepers a Sorrow Stones.

All a' this here accounting come to us Keepers over time, through the whispering in our heads from The Stone Collectors. The rest come ta us in the times when a Keeper be fallen with a sickness a' the body, or the mind. In those dark times Keepers be fighting against letting the Light Stealers whisperings in ta our heads.

We Keepers protect those what take the sorrow from the stones. We protect 'em and humans, from they other half the Light Stealers. We keep 'em from taking the light from the world. We keep 'em from bringing all breathing beings to live down in they dark Tree underworld.

This here be my final account on the beginnings a' things.

Veya closed the journal. A coldness invaded the space around her, even as sweat dripped down her back. *Great, now I'm supposed to buy a twisted fairy tale featuring swamp rats as some kind of other worldly beings?*

Movement in the front yard caught her eye; something white.

Triste?

She stood from the rocker and looked out of the screen door. No white gown, only the gloom of night threatening to enter. Her mind screamed with questions, but her exhausted body needed sleep. Another movement stopped her from entering the house. A silhouette of an animal, or was it human, stood inches from the porch steps. Could it be the swamp rat of her childhood nightmares, or one of the creatures in the journal she'd left abandoned on the rocking chair? Her breath caught at the mere thought before the anger she'd been holding came tumbling out over her fear.

"What do you want?" she yelled, not caring if she woke anyone. By the time she'd unlatched the door and run out into the yard, whatever had been there was gone. Walking back to the porch she began to wonder if she'd actually seen anything at all.

Great, now I'm screaming at nothing. Come on, keep your head clear. Triste needs you. She shut and locked the front door. Then she went, drained of all feeling, to her old bedroom.

Imprisoned by the memories of the many threatening shadows held within the four walls of her childhood room, Veya fell into an uneasy sleep.

Chapter Seven

Veya woke to the smell of chicory coffee and Brin standing in the doorway of the bedroom. "Veya, it's time ta get up. Daylight's waitin' on ya." Her sister's voice mirrored the sound of their mother's when they'd been children and didn't want to get up for school.

She handed Veya the coffee while saying, "We best be gettin' out ta the Tree this mornin'. There be grits waitin' for ya in the kitchen. The rain clouds done started formin'. Daddy says a storm's a'brewin'."

As Veya quickly dressed an apparition of her youth came from the vanity where she'd sat getting ready each morning: Her mother standing behind her combing her hair telling her, *Now you know child, never leave your hair anywhere. Always clean your brush and bury the hair or float it in the bayou. You don't want no one conjuring on you with your own hair or nail clippings, do ya? They's powerful juju in what be shed from your own body.*

She picked up the hairbrush lying on the vanity and roughly, not caring about the pain, attempted to detangle the knots in her hair. The mere thought of having forgotten the true reason behind her strange ritual tick of always cleaning her hairbrush, and flushing the hair strands down the toilet, annoyed her. *Damn, I do the same thing with my nail clippings.* She searched for other odd impulses engrained in her, and found when out camping and on her monthly she'd always dug a hole in the earth to dispose of the tampons or pads. She'd never thrown them in the garbage like a normal person would.

To add to her annoyance, Veya had woken with the dreaded *gray* of Triste's world clasped unyielding on to her.

She dug her cell phone out of her bag, surprised to see she had service, and immediately called the hospital. Dr. Ming explained he'd ordered more tests to determine how Triste's organs were being affected. *Affected? What he really means is shutting down. Why the hell doesn't he just say it? Say, dying?*

After finishing her call with Dr. Ming, she called Daniel. He assured her Triste rested comfortably when he'd checked on her after his shift the evening before. He then reassured her he'd just gone home to change clothes, and would be back to sleep by Triste's side until he had to return to work.

With a few bites of cheesy grits in her stomach, and her phone calls completed, Veya entered her mother's room. A mental picture resembling an old double negative photo of Marie wavered over Triste lying in her hospital bed. The thought of either of them dying hit Veya like a bullet—an invasive thing which remained lodged in her chest, unable to be removed.

With images of death imbedded within her, she left the room and went in search of Brin. She found her once again on the porch. She had questions. If Brin wanted her to go anywhere near the infernal Tree hidden deep in the Island's marshes, she'd first have to answer Veya's questions.

A memory unearthed by a single session with a hypnotherapist held bits and pieces of a time when, as a child, Veya had followed her mother to the Tree. She'd never wanted to see beyond the fear exhumed by the one session, so the Tree remained an illusion. A thing which existed solely through the eccentric beliefs of the Islanders, her mother, and now Brin. But now Veya had dreams and visions of Triste all of which featured a tree. Could it the same tree?

Veya had managed to say, "Brin, I need—" before her sister interrupted and started speaking.

"Dr. Mary's already been ta see 'bout Mamma while daylight waited on you to wake up. She's goin' ta the hospital ta make arrangements. Says Mamma be needin' some more testin' done. She'll be back in the mornin'. I'm afraid, Veya. You know Mamma'd rather die than be taken off the Island." In a whisper she repeated, "She'd rather die."

Ever the logical older sister Veya started to reason with her. "Brin, you must know it's for the best …"

Brin glared up at Veya from the rocking chair daring her to finish the sentence and said, "I been thinkin' on it. If I can get in 'ta the Tree, maybe I can find a Mortlin'."

Veya grabbed on to the sentence her sister had just uttered. "There. That. What do you mean *in* the Tree? It's one thing for me to believe any of these things even exist. But to believe there's some other world inside a Tree, and the thing our mother told me about who talks to her, the swamp rat, is real? How … how can I believe any of it?"

"You'll see, you'll see the truth a' it all. The Mortlin' could help me get Triste's and Mamma's stones back. I know some a' the words a Keeper be sayin' when they place a stone in the Tree ta release the sadness the stone's owner be carryin'. I don't know if'n placin' the stones in the Tree will unbind Mamma and Triste's sorrow, enough to wake them. But I gotta try."

"Unbind their sorrow? Is that what you think? They're in some kind of catatonic state because of depression? Damn, Brin. I came here thinking … I don't know what the hell I was thinking. Maybe I thought you or Mamma had some tonic to wake Triste. But this other stuff is plain lunacy. I've treated many people for depression and none, I repeat none, of them ever went into a coma, or catatonic state. The work Dr. Ming says he's doing? I've never heard of it."

Brin stood from the rocker, and said, "Well now, Veya, was any a' those folks a St. James woman, or an Islander? Probably not, I'm a'thinkin'."

Without waiting for Veya to respond Brin continued, "We St. James women, we gots other reasonings for the stones we wear. The stone, what a Mortlin' gives us when we placed overnight at the Tree for they blessin' after we birthed. I don't be knowin' what all the reasonings be, but I got a knowin' they exist. So, I be countin' mightily on a Mortlin' tellin' me how ta use the stones ta release your Triste and our mamma from they deep sleep. I only been in the Tree once with Mamma, and—"

Veya interrupted her, "You've been to the Tree? Tell me about it."

Brin looked up as the first drops of rain hit the tin roof of the house. "It be another story ta tell at another time, and now ain't it. The storm's a startin' ta kick up. You can come with me or not. But if'n ya comin' ya best be askin' Daddy for his rain slicker, and don't forget your stone." Brin looked directly at the watch normally hidden under Veya's clothes and said, "Never mind I see ya got it."

Veya looked down at the pendent lying at the center of the V cut into her blue *Keep Talking, I'm Diagnosing You* t-shirt. "What? This is Grandmamma's old watch, not a stone. Are you seeing things? I threw my stone in the bayou years ago. I actually don't own a stone of any kind." She lifted her hands so her sister could see the one ring she wore, given to her by Triste. The silver band with a crescent moon etched in it held no stone. A small worry started to grow at the thought of her sister going alone to the Tree.

Brin reached for the watch pendant and held it between two fingers. "Yes, I remember the watch. Can ya take it off so I can look at it closer?"

Veya unclasped the necklace and handed it to Brin. The worry over her sister's grasp of reality grew. Before Veya could follow her Brin had entered the house and come back out holding the necklace and a screwdriver. She placed the necklace on the small table sitting beside their mother's rocker. "Ya know I loved Grandmamma too and I never got anythin' of hers when she died. I pestered Mamma so much, she finally told me I could have Grandmamma's rosary. 'Course she never give it to me. Now she says she can't find it." Brin gripped the screwdriver, slipping its square head on the lip of the watch's back plate.

Veya reached to stop whatever Brin intended to do with her pendant. "So what? You're going to destroy my necklace, because you're jealous?" But before she could intervene Brin had accomplished her goal and popped the watch's back off.

Veya's body vibrated with disbelief when Brin tilted the watch sideways and a white stone the size of a quarter tumbled out, identical to Brin's. Veya stuttered, "That … that's … not … possible. How did that get in there? It must be another stone. It can't be mine! Maybe Grandmamma's stone? It's not mine! Mine is at the bottom of the swamp, or in some gator's gullet." The words had no sooner escaped her mouth when she recalled the cord she'd found before her plane had departed Ashland. Her knees buckled. Her mother's rocker stood directly behind her, catching her fall.

Brin didn't put the stone back in its hiding place as she carefully snapped the watch's back in place. Instead, she took the stone with the loop of silver fastened to its top, strung it on the chain, and hung the necklace back around Veya's neck. Dropping the watch pendent into Veya's lap she said, "If you're comin' with me ya best get movin'."

Veya looked down at the watch and then to the stone. It took several moments before her legs were steady enough to hold her upright. Every instinct she had told her not to follow Brin out to the Tree. At the same time, every protective intuition she'd developed since the moment she'd looked in Triste's newborn eyes, told her she had no choice. She tucked the watch in her jeans pocket and went into the house to get ready. She would follow her sister out to the woods and to the Tree. The Tree, where fear waited for her with the face of a swamp rat.

❧

They moved in silence with Veya following behind Brin. Fortunately, the covering of trees shielded them from the brunt of their constant companion, rain. Through its monotonous drip, drip Veya lost all track of time. They cut through underbrush and ducked to avoid branches hanging thick with gray-green moss while traversing what passed as the trail. Their matching black galoshes at times were sucked up to their ankles in the marsh. Veya's legs ached with each effort to pull a foot free without losing the rubber boot to the muck of the Island. Her gaze perpetually searched the ground for the next bog.

When a long patch of ground in front of her appeared safe, she hazarded a look up and there *it* was—The Tree. It did indeed exist. *Does that mean the creatures do too?*

The size of it made her question why she'd not seen at least a glimpse of its canopy sooner. It was as though an invisible force field had shielded it until the moment she looked up.

Even at a distance of roughly six-city blocks away, its canopy loomed above and past them like some prehistoric monster from another world—a world where dinosaurs roamed, a world void of human beings. If its branches were hollow, the inside would be as large as the tunnels she'd driven through burrowed in the side of mountains. The branches protruded out at least three city-blocks before drooping so far down in places they touched the ground. The smaller limbs at the ends of the massive branches curled in, giving them the illusion of being colossal hands trying to burrow into the earth. The trees around it were dwarfed by its size, tiny toys in comparison.

When she pulled her gaze away from the canopy a wide expanse of water surrounding the Tree's base came into view. A rope bridge spanned the distance, from pilings pounded into the ground on the Island to one of the Tree's many large roots. The bridge dangled precariously over the murky water. She realized they'd have to cross the swaying thing to reach the Tree where Brin said they would find the inside entrance. She walked slowly toward the bridge.

Veya, pondering the absurd idea of actually entering the Tree, inspected the bridge further. *Is it rope?* Pulling her gaze from the bridge she looked up at the Tree's crown again. Its upper most branches disappeared in the angry storm clouds, heavy with rain. The Tree's oscillating branches moved through the dark churning clouds, giving the appearance of the Tree creating the storm by the sheer movement of its limbs. No matter how far back she craned her head she couldn't see where the Tree's canopy ended. Looking for Brin, she found her standing on the bridge a few feet ahead staring fixedly at the Tree.

There were no leaves on the Tree's thrashing branches. *Is it dead?* She turned to ask Brin, but instead followed where her sister, with a worried expression on her face, stared. Brin's gaze was fixed on where Veya assumed the entrance would be.

The bridge swung erratically in the increasing wind, presenting a surreal picture. Veya's legs spasmed. Could she force herself to cross it? When she sought her sister out again, worry had been replaced by curiosity on Brin's face. Veya knew her own face, if she could see it, would reveal a mask of filtered terror. Wind wailed around her. She closed her eyes. Before she reopened them, she prayed to a God she did not believe in, that she would find herself dreaming again. She'd wake safe in her bed in Ashland, because none of what she saw could possibly be real.

She opened her eyes. She wasn't dreaming. The bridge continued to rock back and forth sideways from the wind's force. Reluctantly she joined Brin at the bridge's entrance. The pilings connecting it to the Island on either side of her were at least a foot taller than she. The bridge lurched. She grasped tight to the rope railing to keep her balance and a wooden splinter dug deep in the palm of her left hand. The *ropes* weren't ropes, they were actually Tree branches! The Tree's smaller limbs spidering along the ground had intricately interlaced themselves like hundreds of fingers creating a living bridge from the Island to the Tree. The waters of the bayou churning below told her that unless she wanted to chance swimming with moccasins or gators, the bridge was the only way to the Tree.

Standing beside her sister she yelled over the wind's increasing wail, "How in the hell could I have suppressed how huge the thing is, or the bridge?" *Did the Tree intentionally build it? The Tree*! If the Tree were in the redwoods a four-lane highway could easily have been built through its base.

Brin gave Veya a reassuring smile and yelled, "We need ta get 'cross the bridge. It ain't goin' nowhere attached ta the Tree. It be safe. There's an openin' round the back a' the tree. That be the way Mamma and me got in, but the water be higher than when we come. I hope it ain't so far up it be coverin' the openin'." She stopped trying to yell over the wind and motioned with her hand that they'd have to walk around the gnarled roots of the base after they crossed the bridge.

Veya clutched the rough bark of the railing, wishing she'd worn gloves as more slivers of wood attempted to wedge into her skin. Her breath quickened with each snap of a branch or twig flung by the wind through the bridge's tightly woven web of living limbs. They were halfway across when Veya spotted the glint of a stone pounded in the bark of the Tree. There were hundreds of them. Stones of every color were embedded in its bark, forming a pattern. As she focused on the stones, and the pattern they created, her memory threw her back to sitting with the therapist who'd hypnotized her.

The woman had said, "I promise I'll stop if necessary."

An angry child's voice, Veya's voice, responded, "I seen her with a creature! They not real! They just swamp rats, ain't they?"

A Tree branch caught on Veya's left pant leg, scraping her ankle and bringing her back to reality. When she reached down to loosen it, another branch caught in her hair, lacing itself under the hood of her slicker. "What the hell?" She looked up to yell at Brin to help her. But Brin … *Oh dear God, Brin!*

Brin, no longer on the bridge, hung about a foot above it, caught in the Tree's branches. The Tree's limbs wound around her body, wrapping her like a mummy leaving only her face visible, while also lifting her higher and higher above the bridge. The image of the tarot card she'd pulled from Triste's purse lay like translucent velum over her sister's hanging body. A mirror image. Her grandmamma's soft voice seemed to ride on the wind rushing around her, *"Telling cards will always show us what we be needin' ta know."*

Veya saw no movement, no struggle from her sister. Brin's closed eyes gave no hint of life. "NO, Brin!" was all Veya managed to say before a branch caught her at the waist and pulled her up and off the bridge.

Since stepping foot on the Island, Veya had expected to have another episode of panic. After all, they were created by and began on the Island. She no longer had to wait. Dangled several feet above the bridge, the tighter the branches wrapped themselves around her, the more her chest constricted. Her breathing came in great gulps, and the edges of her vision darkened. She'd never wished in all her life to pass out cold, she'd fought against it so many times even knowing she'd never actually pass out. But this time, she wished, no, prayed with all she had, to enter an oblivion of nothingness. The Tree continued weaving, a branch at a time, encasing her body and lifting her toward its canopy in the storm clouds.

But what would become of Triste if she succumbed, or worse yet, died? A new resolve spread with each constricting branch.

No, I will not give in.

When the branches ceased their upward movement, she faced the outside bark of the Tree. She struggled to move, to get a sense of what was happening. The Tree shook. An ear-piercing clamor began above her. She looked up. The bark split open as though hit by a lightning bolt. Along the fissures of the opening the Tree seemed to bleed a rainbow of gem-encrusted colors while Veya struggled against the bonds of the limbs. The stone hanging from her neck, plastered against her skin by the mummy encasement of branches, burned hot. The floating white apparition she'd seen outside the screened porch the night before appeared from within the murky shadows inside the opening of the Tree. A voice came from where it floated, "Mamma! Find the stone, Mamma. Find my stone!"

The Tree's branches reversed their movement, unwrapping from her body while pushing her through its newly formed gaping maw.

A voice, Triste's voice, called out, "Mamma!"

Veya fell. Her head hit something hard before her body crumpled to the ground. Everything around her spun to black.

Chapter Eight

Veya awoke in complete darkness with the right side of her face pressed against a jagged rock. She reached up expecting her skull to have been cracked open and instead fingered an egg-sized knot. Rolling from her side onto her back sent pulsing shots of pain to cascade down her face. Blood from a cut beside the knot had already caked to her hair. Her body dripped with sweat. The wind had eased the heat during her and Brin's walk to the Tree. She no longer felt a breeze. Warmth baked the ground where she'd landed.

Inside.

She was inside the Tree! The silence surrounding her was far worse than the raging storm she'd been pulled from.

She tried to sit up, but her aching head forced her back down. She called out, her voice just above a whisper. "Brin, are you here?"

Somewhere in the distance, water trickled. Brin didn't respond. She carefully tried to sit up again. The cut on her head opened and blood dripped down her face. Her stomach heaved. Bile spewed from her mouth mixed with the coppery taste of blood. She moved her arms and legs to see if bones were broken. They were sore, but still intact with only scratches on the parts of bare skin where the branches had wound.

"Brin?" She called out again. No answer. She reached in her jeans pocket for her cell phone. It would provide at least some light, but as she withdrew it she felt its shattered face. It'd been destroyed.

The movement of her hand searching the ground around her loosened dirt from the jagged-edged rock her head had hit. She continued to remove any dirt still clinging to its hot, red surface.

Red? Hot? Light?

Confused, she scraped away the last layers of dirt to reveal a crystalline stone about twelve inches in circum-ference. Once uncovered, the light coming from within it cast a crimson haze in a circle of several feet around her. Tree roots wound along the packed dirt where the light shown. She strained to see beyond the light. An object lay still at the edge of its beam. Head pulsing, she crept toward the mound. The nearer she came to it the more panic crawled with her.

Brin lay face down, motionless. Veya reached out and shook her, desperate to determine if she was alive or dead.

Relief crashed through Veya when Brin lifted her muck-covered face, and said, "Well, I guess I don't have ta figure no more on how ta get in ta the Tree."

Veya, unmoved by her sister's attempt at humor, said, "Great, but how do we get *out* of it? Do you have any idea where we are? Are you okay?" In the gloom beyond the glow of the stone she heard something move. "Did you hear that?" Veya wiped at the blood still dripping from the wound on her head.

Brin sat up. "I don't think I broke anythin', just scraped up a bit. What 'bout you? You're a bleedin'. Let's get closer ta that red light so I can take a look at it."

They stood, resting on each other for support, walked to the circle of light, and sat down in its comforting glow. Despite her protests Brin began inspecting Veya's head. Her searching gentle hands were cool against Veya's overheated skin. "Yep, you got yourself a right big egg there, but I don't be sensin' anythin' gone wrong in your head." She continued the light touch, fingers caressing the knot. Veya relaxed; the throbbing eased. Brin began to hum in such a deep cadence its vibration filled Veya's own body. By the time Brin removed her hands, Veya had no idea how much time had passed. When she felt her head, the knot was gone. A faint raised line was the only evidence she'd hit her head, or that a cut had ever existed.

She managed a hoarse, "Thank you." For once, she didn't ask the questions piling in her brain. Had her sister performed some kind of miracle? She hoped Brin could do the same for Triste.

Brin smiled a knowing grin and said, "Mamma brought me in ta the Tree the week 'afore I found her with them two dead Mortlins. Least I think they be dead. I went back ta bury 'em the day after and they wasn't there no more." Her eyes scanned the area around them and she continued. "Only, when she brung me we went through an openin' round the other side a' tha Tree, down below, at its base. We wasn't picked up and dropped in through its top."

Veya marveled at her sister's ability to accept what had just happened to them as though it were no more than a daily occurrence.

Brin crossed her legs, laid her hands on her knees palms up, and closed her eyes. Veya thought for a moment her sister was going to meditate. She opened her mouth to comment on the absurd timing, when Brin began talking again. "I don't know how much I should be tellin' ya 'bout Keepers and they ways. But a Keeper only comes in ta the inside a' the Tree three times in they life. The first time be when they be brought ta the heart center a' the Tree by the old Keeper, ta see if'n the Hadlins be acceptin' them as they new Keeper. Ya see over time the Keepers be realizin' that they power be stronger if not just the Mortlins be acceptin' 'em, but the Hadlins too. I reckon it be 'cause the stones be give ta the Tree, and the Hadlins be the ones what take care a' the Tree. The second time is when the Keeper be gettin' on in age and bringin' the new Keeper for the ascendin' rites. The last time is when the old Keeper dies. The new Keeper gots ta bring the dead Keeper's stone inta the Tree, and place the stone along the path ta the Tree's heart center. This here red stone was an old Keeper's stone. It were once the size a' mine and yours. The small stone be dug in ta the Tree's root, and as the Tree grows it grows too. "

Veya paused at the outlandish thought of a stone growing, but decided against the argument, and instead asked, "So is that why Mamma brought you in the Tree, so you could ascend and be the next Keeper? What happened, and what does this have to do with Triste?"

Brin looked into Veya's eyes then turned away. For a moment Veya thought her sister wasn't going to answer her. But Brin, with her gaze fixed toward the black void beyond the stone's glow said, "All I be knowin' is Mamma wouldn't talk ta me 'bout anythin' after we left the Tree. They be things I can tell ya and they be things ya gots ta learn on your own. That be what Mamma told me, and that be what I be tellin' you. My head be a spinnin'. Doin' a healin', like I just done on ya, do take some out a' me."

From the direction of where Brin still stared there came a scraping sound, like something being dragged. Veya started to ask what the noise causing the hair on her arms to lift might be. The thought fled when her sister's necklace burst from within, flashing a vibrant white light.

What? She reached for her own necklace. The stone, warm to the touch, also emitted a silver-white beam. She jumped when the sound of dragging became grating, something hit or being torn apart a long distance away. At least she hoped it was far away. She hated the pleading tone in her voice when she asked Brin, "Why are our necklaces now glowing?"

Brin sighed, and as though talking to a child said, "Didn't Mamma ever tell ya nothin' 'bout our ways? No, 'cause ya didn't want ta listen. Our stones will give off light if'n a Mortlin' or Hadlin' be anywhere near us."

"They're here? Is that what that sound is? Have you tried to talk to them? Why haven't we seen them?" Veya's questions tumbled out as she attempted to keep her voice from betraying the fear behind the words. She'd spent her entire childhood avoiding seeing the creatures her mother spoke of and now, now she encouraged her sister to bring one out into the open?

Brin's *why are you so stupid* voice cut through Veya. "Some Mortlins always be near the Tree, and the Hadlins always been livin' inside a' it. But I done already told ya they *all* inside a' it now."

Veya shuddered at the thought of what could be in the abyss surrounding them. The dragging had been replaced with a pounding like rock against rock echoing around her. Her legs twitched. They wanted to run, but to where? Instead she stood up and reached down to help Brin stand again. Her sister's needy grip cut off the circulation in Veya's hand, and it took several attempts before Brin could stand on her own unattended.

Concerned, Veya asked, "Are you okay? Are we in any kind of danger? I mean we were just dumped here by a Tree!"

"I be fine, and the Tree knows better than ta hurt us."

"Great, a tree with knowing. What the hell? Never mind. What's the plan now that we are *in* the Tree? How do we find a Mortling? You said one must be nearby, since our stones are glowing, and what is this heart center? Is it where we find Triste and Mamma's stones?"

Veya breathed heavily. She didn't know if her labored breath was caused from the lack of air in the tree, or the fact they were inside the Tree! She knew she asked too many questions, or questions her sister couldn't, or wouldn't, answer, so she added, "Sorry, I know I'm asking too many questions."

Brin had walked to the edge of the light, and peered into the shadows.

"No, they not too many just some I can't be answerin', and I been tryin' to figure on a plan. When Mamma brought me in, we didn't have ta follow the path lit by the old Keepers' way stones ta the heart center, 'cause the openin' we come through is where the heart center be."

Something being dragged again caught Veya's attention, as the musky scent of the perfume her mother wore drifted past her. She waited to see if Brin reacted to either. When Brin said nothing, she decided her own nervous mind was playing tricks on her. She asked, "So how far are we from this heart center?"

Brin again sighed. "I got no knowin' on how far down the heart center be. When Mamma took me ta it, there be no Hadlin' there and none ever come ta accept me as they new Keeper. So I never seen the old Keepers' Way Stones lit up on the path going up ta the top a' the Tree. Mamma and me, we went back home, and she started a'readin' all the past Keepers' teachings. Like I done said she wouldn't talk ta me 'bout it. I figure she be hopin' it'd happened 'afore, and the book would tell her what ta do. So you and me just gonna have ta start walkin' down and hope we find more Way Stones ta guide us. "

The sound of dragging stopped, replaced by clicking. Veya envisioned claws tapping a hard surface.

"What the hell is that?" Veya turned in a circle trying to determine where the noise came from. When she turned back to Brin the only light she could see was that cast by their twin necklaces.

The red light was gone.

They were enveloped in pitch black again.

Brin's face, aglow from the light of her necklace, stared, transfixed in the direction of where the stone had shone as though willing its light to come back.

It didn't.

Veya panicked at the thought of being in the dark with nothing other than the small beam hanging from her neck and pulled a tissue out of her pocket to wipe the sweat dripping down the base of her neck. A card came with the tissue. She caught it in mid-air as it passed before her eyes. *Where the hell did this come from?* She moved her hand to feel the bulge of the pouch of stones she'd taken with her in the front pocket of her jeans. *But I didn't take the cards. Did I?* She thought back to the night before when she'd taken the deck out to look more closely at each card. *Maybe I did take this one.* The light of her necklace reflected off the drawing etched on the thin cardboard rectangle, a human body with a skeletal face. The body was pierced through with swords and knives. An ax was wedged in its back and yet the gruesome body still stood upright. Her grandmamma's words of so long ago whispered through her mind yet again. *The cards, they always gots somethin' ta tell ya.* Before hurling the worrisome image out into the abyss surrounding her she wondered, *What the hell is this telling me?* The clicking sounds began again. This time the image of claws were replaced in Veya's mind with swords and knives.

Brin, who hadn't seen the vile telling card, calmly said, "We'll have ta use our small stones ta see by 'til we find the next way stone. If I be goin' by what is writ in the Keepers' book there be at least seven way stones before we get ta the heart center. Come on, we gots ta get goin'. Your Triste ain't got much time left, and I figure Mamma's got less."

Veya started to ask Brin how she could possibly know about the length of time Triste or their mamma had left. But the foreboding of the telling card combined with Brin walking away, unnerved her.

She followed behind her sister as they left the spot where the red stone had glowed. The farther they walked the more acutely Veya felt the cloying misery of the *gray*.

They ventured through the obscure unknown with only enough light to see mere inches around them. Veya's mind screamed, *No, stay, stay, the light might come back on*. But she continued moving. With each step taken the solid foundation she'd built, the life she'd fashioned for herself and Triste, crumbled a bit more. She now clung to the thought that Triste, or some part of her, was out there, and that somehow she could help her.

The clicking continued to resonate around them as she followed behind Brin's silhouette, whose edges sparked occasionally with the white luminescent glow created by the stone hanging at her neck. Down, Brin had said they'd be going down. But how? Trees were solid inside, weren't they? Of course, trees didn't have glowing stones either. Seven stones her sister had said. She hoped they'd find the next one soon and why hadn't the creatures shown themselves? So many questions to ponder while walking toward something she didn't believe in.

Chapter Nine

Veya took off her father's rain slicker and tied its sleeves around her waist. The Tree pulsated with a stifling heat. Why hadn't she taken the sweat-incubating slicker off sooner? Brin stood a few feet from her waiting impatiently and started walking away as soon as Veya was done. It occurred to Veya that Brin had been the reason she'd not removed the piece of clothing earlier. She needed her sister, something she hated admitting to herself. She had no reassurance Brin wouldn't walk off and leave her to the darkness. That thought, and the mind numbing clicking, had her nerves sparking like firecrackers.

The monotony of following Brin increased the weight of misery that had followed Veya from Triste's hospital bed. The eternal void crept around her like an ominous beast waiting to swallow her whole. When a faint light appeared in the distance, she first thought the shimmer to be a hallucination. But no matter how often she closed her eyes and looked again, the light remained. She hesitantly questioned Brin, "Do you see it? The light?"

"Yes, I seen the way stone long 'afore you did." Brin's voice, mere inches from Veya sounded miles away. "She said we be comin' up on it."

"She? Who's she?" Hope sprang from Veya's dark cocoon. "Are you talking to a Mortling? I thought they were androgynous?"

"No, it ain't been no Mortlin' talkin' ta me, and yes they not be needin' another bein' ta birth a new one."

Brin kept going, having answered only one part of the question. Who was *she?* Veya was tired of Brin's half answers so she reached out to stop her sister's forward movement, and caught at air instead. The absence of light had impaired her depth perception. Brin was much further away than Veya perceived.

Frustrated, Veya yelled, "Stop! What are you saying? You said you'd find a Mortling and they'd talk to you. If it's not a Mortling then who is *she* and why haven't you told me?"

Veya kept walking not realizing Brin had stopped. Once again, her vision distorted her perception. She hit her sister's back, full force, knocking them both to their knees. Crouched together, the erratic swaying of their necklaces cast a faint light not only on their faces, but for brief moments toward the outer deep pockets of darkness.

Veya saw *it* before Brin did. She grabbed her stone, turning its light toward where she'd seen two red spots.

Eyes?

The stone's slight beam caught the glint of crimson again as the body of the creature with red eyes stepped from the shadows and into the light.

Veya slowly stood while the creature moved further out of the shelter of darkness. For a never-ending moment her eyes were locked with the creature's. She turned to run, and once again thought, *where can I go?*

The creature stood not two feet from them, motionless, other than its one claw tapping at something on its chest.

Its red eyes held her gaze; this thing, this illusion, this creature her mother valued above all else. It moved until it stood mere inches from her, the swamp rat that lurked, an evil shadow, in every one of her nightmares. It had taken her many therapy sessions to transform the creature from its leathery, horn-eared, rat-tailed self, to simply a large swamp rat. After transforming it, it had taken even longer for the swamp rat to cease chasing her in her dreams, and now here the monster stood, living and breathing. Not a swamp rat, not the fantasies of a small child, but the true other-worldly creature itself. It was real!

The claw, something she did not recall from her nightmares, protruded from an index finger twice as long as her own. The thing's other five, leathery rodent digits were a good inch shorter than its index finger. The claw never ceased its incessant tapping on the skull of a small creature, perhaps a bird, that hung from its neck on a string made of the same bark rope as the bridge. Inside the skull a stone resembling an ember of coal blazed.

Brin stood up next to her, and without a remote tinge of fear in her voice said, "I never seen one 'afore, but it be a Hadlin'. Come on, let's keep goin'."

"Keep going? Wait! Can it … can it hurt us? You said it would help us." Veya grabbed her sister, stopping her from leaving.

Brin shook her off, and shone the light of her stone toward the creature's red eyes as another rat-like thing with white eyes came out of the inky depths and stood next to it. "It ain't gonna do nothin' ta us 'cause the Mortlin' there won't let it. See how the Mortlin's eyes be a different color? It's how I know the difference. Didn't ya read what I give ya on the beginning a' things?" Brin pointed to the white-eyed thing and continued. "I done waited ta see if'n the Mortlin' would mind whisper ta me, but it didn't."

Solid white slits stared at Veya. The same rawhide skin of the red-eyed creature surrounded the other's bright eye sockets. Moist skin sagged from below the two holes where a nose should've been down to its neck. Did the loose skin hide some hideous maw of a mouth? Veya didn't want to know.

Brin began to once again walk away, then as though remembering something she stopped and said, "Best watch your step as we be gettin' closer ta the next lighted stone ya seen. I figure we be startin' ta go down along the

Way soon. I know from some a' what Mamma taught me parts a' the Tree be underwater at times. I got no way a knowin' where we actually be in the Tree, so the storm outside might be bringin' on some water."

As though on cue, a keening wind swirled down from above, twisting, a tornado come to life. The gale pulled at Veya, threatening her balance. Then as quickly as the strong gust had appeared it dissipated upward.

Veya imagined having to swim in the snake-infested waters of the bayou. "We're high enough in the Tree to be out of the water for now, aren't we?"

Brin continued on saying, "Ya never know in a storm how high the water will get, and as I recall ya be a pretty good swimmer."

Veya looked at the Hadling and Mortling. The Hadling lifted the hand not tapping the bird skull. Thick mucus oozed from its palm.

She hurried after Brin.

The click, click of talon on bone followed at her heals. *Is it following me?*

Brin walked while saying, "It be Mamma that's been a talkin' ta me. Mamma always be a talkin' ta me, ever since her body went ta sleep."

Veya, struggling to comprehend what she was seeing, barely heard Brin. She had turned to make certain the creatures were not following, and was relieved to see they weren't. Instead, they were locked in what appeared to be an embrace, but as they moved, she realized they were struggling against each other.

"Are they fighting?"

As the words escaped her mouth, the tapping of thousands of claws hitting bone came from out of the void behind them, and the white spark of two eyes locked on to hers. In her mind she heard—*help us*. Then the two creatures, in unison, faded into the darkness that echoed with the clamor of talons on bone.

She turned from the din to find her sister no longer near her.

Veya's worry of losing what little grip she had left on reality caught up to her when she reached Brin. She hesitantly asked, "Mamma? It's Mamma telling you where to go?"

"Well, it be Mamma tellin' me what the Mortlin' be tellin' her. Only Mamma says the Mortlin's not in its right mind. There be somethin' wrong with it."

Veya was unable to respond to this new revelation because the ground had begun slanting downward, and the incline got progressively steeper. She had to pay close attention to every step she took.

The orange light they'd been moving toward showed itself in an elongated stream of flashes. Ahead of her Brin veered away from the light while looking down and stopping every so often.

When she reached Brin she understood what her sister was doing. The Tree's branches had dropped them onto a large rock shelf embedded in the wall of the tree. The shelf tilted sharply down. The orange shimmering way stone, the beacon which they had been navigating toward, was not straight ahead, but to their right and below where they stood.

She mimicked Brin's movements, edged nearer to the ledge's rim, and peered over. To her left, darkness loomed. To her right and below, the orange way stone flickered. Viewing it from above and angled, it cast a much brighter glow than they had been following. She tried to calculate the length of the opening between them and the stone below, at least half the size of a football field. She wondered if her vision was once again playing tricks with her mind, because she could not grasp what she was seeing.

The Tree is hollow inside! How can that possibly be and how are we going to get to the stone?

A gust of wind again rushed upon them, but this gust didn't come from above. The gale came from below. Heated fingers coiled around Veya's ankles; looking down, she expected to see the Tree's branches once again enveloping her. There were none. Yet something pulled at her ankles, drawing her toward the abyss between the ledge and the orange Stone below.

The toes of Veya's galoshes hung in midair; her heels had dug trenches in the muddy soil trying to escape the phantom hands attempting to pull her over. With her body teetering on the ledge's rim Veya glimpsed rough cut stairs along the inside of the Tree. Their path led down to the way stone.

How far down will I fall?

Veya, rigid with tension in anticipation of the fall, startled when Brin grabbed her arm and yanked her back. The sensation of hands on her ankles broke away as she fell backward. She sat up and tried to steady her shaking limbs.

Brin stood over her, hands on her hips, and said, "Best ta stand back from the edge, the squalls comin' from the storm have a power in 'em. Don't want the strong current ta take ya down. Best ta walk there on your own."

Anger replaced Veya's fear. "Something was pulling me, trying to take me over the ledge."

Brin reached down to help her up. "It just be the wind. We best be stickin' close ta the walls a' the Tree as we be makin' our way down."

Veya refused her sister's outstretched hand. She found she couldn't move. Her skin seemed to crawl on her bones. Something had tried to pull her over the edge. Fingers had wrapped around her leg, not wind. There was a rip in her pants leg around her ankle where the sensation of the grip still lingered. She pulled the torn fabric aside to see a single line of blood trailing down her calf as though a sharp knife had sliced through her skin. Had a rock carried on the wind caused the cut or a talon attached to a leathery hand trying to pull her to her death?

Brin tore a piece of cloth from the sleeve of her blouse and wrapped the cut to stop the bleeding. "Cut's not too deep. It'll heal right up," were her sister's few words of comfort before they began again.

Veya didn't have the energy to argue, or to not continue. She stood and followed Brin.

When they reached the first of the steps Veya had seen as she teetered on the edge, she hesitated. The stairs leading off of the ledge and to the orange way stone were narrow, barely wide enough to stand sideways on. Brin placed her hand on Veya's shoulder. "I'm thinkin' they be many a' these we need ta be takin' 'afore we get ta where we goin'."

Veya stepped down onto the first stair.

One.

She clung to the Tree's bark afraid the wind would return, or she'd slip into oblivion off the treacherous uneven slabs. She counted each step as her foot inched along, and moved downward to the next one. Some were chiseled-out indentions in the Tree's bark. Others were miniature versions of the rock ledge they'd been dropped on, protruding from the inner bark of the Tree.

Have we been in here for hours or mere minutes?

By the time she could talk with a steady voice they were halfway to the orange glow. She'd counted seventy-five steps. She tried to formulate the impossible question she knew she must ask her sister. The problem being no matter how her sister answered the question, Brin would sound crazy.

Am I really going to follow an unstable person through a hole in the middle of a tree filled with—what—following us? What are they? Where did they come from? Good God, listen to yourself. What about your own sanity?

She took a deep breath.

Ask the damn question.

"Why didn't you tell me Mamma was talking to you? How, how can she be talking to you and a Mortling when she's … she's not here, Brin."

Veya stopped, breathing in the earthy cedar scent of the Tree's damp bark to which she clung, and said, "She's barely alive."

Brin stopped and looked up at Veya. She wore the shiny smile Veya remembered her using when she wanted to get her way as a child—*Veya please buy me some candy, give a ride on your shoulders, play dolls with me, please Veya.*

With the smile still plastered to her face Brin responded, "Mamma didn't never want me tellin' ya. She knowed ya wouldn't believe me. You'd think I be like her, not right in the head. She said, even if by some miracle ya did believe she's a'talkin' ta me … well, she said if the words come from her, you'd have nothin' ta do with 'em. Probably try ta talk me out a' believin' myself."

Veya, always ready to dispute anything their mother espoused, argued, "Now wait a minute, just because I've never been interested, who cares? You always were. But I mean, you have to know this is all, well, crazy? Yes?"

The smile faded from Brin's face. "Ya seen the Mortlin' and Hadlin'. Ya seen the Tree and the way stones. I don't got no more ta give ya. Now ya got ya own daughter mixed in ta ya fightin' against Mamma."

Something she'd seldom felt invaded Veya's senses—guilt. Could she be responsible for Triste's illness?

No, it's Mamma's doing.

They continued moving, but Veya needed this argument. She spoke to Brin while still clinging for life at each step her foot descended upon. "Don't you dare, don't you dare bring Triste into this and blame me for it. If anyone is to blame it's Mamma. How many times did I ask her to be a normal mother? How many times did I beg her to leave this god-forsaken piece of dirt in the middle of nowhere? And when you were born so soon after our baby brother Billy died, you were all she needed. Little Miss Merry Sunshine. You followed her around like a lost puppy." Veya's already unsteady, nervous body pumped with wave upon wave of red-hot anger, but the guilt had taken hold too, and watched from the sidelines.

Veya stepped on the last indentation before they reached the orange way stone and counted, *Two Hundred.*

The orange way stone, twice the size of the red stone, was buried in a Tree root on a ledge barely large enough for the two of them to stand facing each other. It sparked ambers at its center and lighter tinges of pale, yellow oranges around its edges, creating an illusion of fire burning within its crystalline interior.

Brin moved to stand over the stone while responding to Veya's accusations. "Mamma said you blamed her for the death a' the baby brother birthed 'afore me. I got no knowin' of a time before my birthin'. All I know is Mamma said you never give your sorrow ta the Tree. She said you kept the stone she give ya ta take away your sadness over him dyin'. Why would you do such a thing?"

Veya stared into the stone's center. "When Mamma had Billy, I was eight years old, and loved being his big sister, his protector. I woke the morning after he died— I've always assumed he died from what is now called SIDS—to Mamma stirring up grits for breakfast. She put the bowl in front of me, and like reporting no more than the weather she said, 'Your brother died last night. Your Daddy and I done buried him this mornin'. Here's your stone. I be takin' ya out ta the Tree when ya done with your breakfast.'"

Looking from the stone out to the ebony surrounding them, Veya shouted, "The Tree, always the damn Tree and her *practices*." Her voice echoed around them. She lowered her voice, and continued. "I ran to his room. He was three months old. His empty crib still smelled of the sweet baby powder clinging to the blankets. I remember I held the stone in my hand so tight its rough edges cut my palm. When Mamma came looking for me later in the day I told her I wasn't giving away Billy. The stone became my way of remembering him. I carried it until the day before I left the Island, then I gave that damn stone to the swamp."

"But that ain't right. Ya was supposed to …"

Veya moved away from the comfort of the glistening way stone. "I don't give a damn about what she thought I should do." She looked around for another stone to guide their way. Beyond the flickering sparks and past the ledge, there were more steps. She walked over to inspect them. They repeated the same pattern as those they'd just traversed, spiraling down along the cavity of the Tree's wall, and disappearing in the black void below them. She found no light to guide them. "There's no way I'm going down those. We could fall." Fear and anger mingled with a familiar tightening of her chest.

Panic.

Her old friend wanted to pay a visit.

Brin pointed out into the void and said, "The way stones be down those steps. So yes, this be the way we goin'. I think I can see the next stone. Ya see the tiny flick a yellow?"

Veya saw nothing. "For all I know it's another Hadling or Mortling waiting to shove me off the steps as soon as I get far enough down there. You said there's something wrong with the Mortlings. Aren't we depending on them to help us? Wait, Brin. Stop!"

Her sister had once again left her and moved out of sight, saying, "Come on, Veya. Triste be a waitin' for ya. Mamma thinks I can help the Mortlins when we get ta the heart center."

Triste.

Veya thought back to what began the horror where she now lived. Triste standing at the end of her bed, calling out for help. Tears threatened. She gripped the rough bark of the Tree's wall, and stepped down to the next indentation.

With each step down she expected to hear a creature below, or see one descending from above. The glow cast by the orange way stone slowly faded until only the faint light cast by her necklace's stone remained.

Water dripped in the distance. She hoped her mind was playing with her already overwrought imagination. But she was wrong. She distinctly heard water, not dripping, but flowing, and coming from either below them, or outside the Tree's inner wall. She prayed for the latter as she counted movement downward.

She cautioned a look down. She could no longer see her sister. Veya inched her foot to the next step.

Five-hundred thirty-seven.

She tried moving faster in an attempt to catch up with Brin, but her rubber-clad foot slipped from the moisture on the next step. She grabbed at a protruding root. At the next step, her foot again threatened to fly out from under her.

"Brin," she yelled. Holding to another tree root she looked down.

A black hole looked back at her.

No, Brin.

A click, tapping, then another click came from the direction she'd last seen her sister. *Are they signaling one another?*

She yelled again, "Brin?" The name bounced off the Tree's hollow center and reverberated back up. "Brrinnn."

While still clinging to a root she continued, one foot on to the next step, then the next.

Is this five hundred forty or forty-one?

If I'm dreaming, let me wake up now, please.

Chapter Ten

The taste of fear coated Veya's tongue. "Brin?" The name bounced back up once more.

This is insane. What the hell am I doing?

She grabbed at a Tree root above her, determined to stop going down, and go back up. At least there she'd have the light of the orange stone. That is, if it still shone.

She'd force Brin to come looking for her.

But will she?

Her foot touched the first step going back up. She started to count backward when it dawned on her she'd lost all memory of what number the step would be.

Damn!

Brin's voice echoed up to her from somewhere below. "Keep comin' down, Veya. I've reached the next way stone."

Veya hesitated on the step. Her mind wouldn't order itself. But her body, of its own volition, turned and began walking downward even as her mind screamed for her to go back up. She wrestled with the opposing emotions of relief—Brin was still alive—and disappointment—she would continue into the unknown.

She'd inched her way along over a dozen steps before she became confident the new steps held no moisture. Mindlessly she struggled forward. Previously she'd passed the time by counting the steps, but when she tried picking a random number to begin again, the practice brought no comfort. It seemed hours had passed before her sister's yellow-tinged form emerged below her. Brin was stooped over something on the outer edge of a much larger platform than the one that had held the fire-orange way stone they'd left behind. Veya released the breath she hadn't realized she'd been holding.

They'd reached the next way stone.

Its buttery yellow glow made Veya yearn for Ashland on a sunny day, but sunny days always included Triste. There could be no sunshine in Veya's life without Triste safely by her side.

Veya walked to her sister, who was bent over a Mortling. The way stone shed a sickly lemon glow over the creature's prone, green-skinned body.

Brin's right hand rested on the thing's chest while the splayed fingers of her left hand were on its head. Without looking up at Veya she said, "Mamma says this here Mortlin' be dyin'." Its eyes were closed, but its chest still rose and fell. Not dead yet.

Brin lifted the lower section of hanging flesh on its face. She then pulled a water bottle from the bag she carried, and poured the liquid in an inch long slit under the flap. Veya assumed the opening to be the thing's mouth though she saw no lips. Her stomach lurched at the sight.

"Dying? Did the Hadling hurt it?" Not wanting to see it, she stared out into the eternal night hoping to see another glow while also afraid of what might be hidden in the black expanse.

No glow appeared.

Brin answered, "I don't know why it be dying. All I know is I got ta try ta help it."

Veya couldn't sort out her confusing emotions. She'd almost forced Brin to come after her. But in truth, she knew she'd been abandoning Brin, because Brin wouldn't have come back up to find her. The confusion grew, and melded with her not giving a damn whether the Mortling lived or died. When the word describing her emotion surfaced it caught hard in her brain and wound itself around her many justifications—*shame*.

The abnormal feeling increased the already massive weight Veya hadn't managed to shake off.

Shame?

She briefly allowed the foreign feeling to settle. Then she hid shame with all the other emotions she didn't want to visit, and clung more tightly to her familiar shroud of righteousness, and grief.

She'd walked to the ledge's edge where a glint of pale green formed out of the obscurity of the darkness, tearing her away from her cloak of distress. The light sparked, increasing in intensity to her right several yards directly below them.

How didn't I see it before?

The stone sat at the center of yet another platform. The wall of protruding roots above it appeared to slither with jade tinted snakes.

Snakes?

She peered more closely and as she continued staring, a shadow of white emerged in an open niche of the Tree's bark directly behind the emerald stone.

Triste? Or is it another stone?

Moving back to Brin she demanded, "There's something on the ledge with the next way stone. Let's go."

Brin removed her hands from the Mortling and held on to the slicker around Veya's waist, preventing her from leaving. She placed her other hand on the Mortling's head and said, "We got ta stay here so I can see ta the Mortlin'."

"I'm not staying here. You said we had little time. I don't give a damn about that thing."

"We got no choice, Veya. I got ta help it. This here Mortlin' be sent ta make sure we git down without a Hadlin' stoppin' us. Ya got no idea a' what's goin' on here.

I just be understandin' some myself, and tryin' ta piece it all together. Stay put, please, and leave me ta what needs doin'."

Veya had never heard her sister's voice so filled with worry, or was she hearing fear? After Brin released her she sat as far away from them as the platform would allow, pulled out her own water and a granola bar. No need to ignore her rumbling stomach if they were going to stop for a few moments. *It'll only be a few, or I'm going ahead by myself.*

She peered over the edge toward the specter she'd seen. It wasn't a stone. It hovered over the emerald glow of the way stone. *Can the ghostly thing be Triste? Come on, get a grip. She's in Oregon in a hospital bed, or has she died … and it's her spirit?*

No sooner had she allowed the thought than she banished it from her mind. *I'm here, Triste. I'll find a way to make you better.*

She looked away and at her sister. Brin pulled out a bag of stones similar to their mother's, but Brin's bag was blood red where their mother's was purple.

She'd once found a burlap pouch in her grandmamma's dresser drawer while looking for a handkerchief. She'd not understood why the older woman would have a pouch of stones like her mamma's, since she knew her grandmamma used only telling cards when doing a reading, never stones.

When she asked, her grandmamma had explained. "We St. James women, we gots many uses for stones. Don't you forget that now, child." The thought of Grandmamma reaching her hand from the hospital gurney swept a wave of old sadness through her.

Stones, stones, always stones, waiting to be taken to the Tree—to be used to relieve someone's grief. In the home where she'd grown up, covering any available flat surface, there were stones of every shape, color and size.

Her sister arranged the stones on the Mortling's torso in a spiraling circle with the tail pointed toward its head. She'd also placed a card face up over its closed eyes. Veya's curiosity overcame her revulsion, and she slid over to see the card. It was just a glimpse, but she recoiled back so fast her left hip hung off the edge of the shelf when she stopped. The card was identical to what Triste had drawn in her diary—andirons on either side of a path bordered by dense trees and foliage.

Andirons? I've seen those before. Were they on the path today?

As though bidding it into existence, her mind allowed a memory to escape its confinement, and she knew exactly where she'd seen the intricately carved metal edifices. The andirons had not been on the path she and Brin had taken. They'd been on another path leading to the Tree. The trail she'd secretly followed. The one their mother had taken out to the Tree at dawn. That day, a ten-year-old Veya had chosen to follow Marie along winding paths filled with the red glowing eyes of swamp rats.

A young Veya had snuck past andirons while following her mother. The path her mother had taken so long ago was vastly different than the one she and Brin were being forced to traverse. Her mother's path had led them directly to a large opening at the base of the Tree. There had been no bridge to cross, and no Tree limbs cocooned them like mummies. Yet to a child's eyes the opening with the andirons represented not a crack in the Tree's trunk, but the Tree's monstrous mouth ready to devour her. Stones were embedded along the edges of the cavity from the base and going up to its canopy for as far as her young eyes could see. They formed a continuous pattern—the exact pattern Brin placed on the Mortling's dying body.

Veya tugged at the memory while also marveling at the years of therapy she'd undergone. So many hours, so much money spent trying to eradicate, or logically explain, what had occurred the day when she'd so innocently followed her mother. Her mind, normally so quick to be rid of memories of the Island, fought desperately to remember more. But years of walls built would not give way and allow her entry beyond the brief glimpse she'd allowed to escape.

She pointed a trembling finger toward the Mortling's body. "Brin, on the other side of the Tree … the opening you said Mamma took you to … are there stones around the opening? Stones whose patterns are shaped like those you've created here?"

"Yes, that be what the openin' looks like. Why you askin'? How do you …" Brin turned from her and back to the Mortling. "Never mind. I got ta think on what I be knowin' now, and Mamma says I best be tellin' ya 'bout it.

"Most folks believe it be the Keeper what bring sorrow stones ta the Tree, but the Keepers and they family give only they own sorrow ta the Tree. The rest a the stones be given ta a Mortlin' after folks give them over ta a Keeper. Mortlins be the ones what bring the stones placin' 'em in the Tree. Teachins passed ta Keepers tell the reasonin' why. Mortlins be the only creature what can hold a stone filled with such overwhelmin' sorrow, and not be brought down with it. Since they very beginnin' Mortlins never have carried inside they head or they heart, any mournin' or grief. The sadness never enters 'em, never touches 'em."

Brin lifted the card from the Mortling's eyes. Even in the void of their white nothingness, Veya felt gratitude emanating from them. Its hand, which had no claw, traced the stones on its body without moving a single one from where it rested.

A profound relief came over Veya. The Mortling lived. *Why do I care?* Disturbed by the feeling she focused onward. "It's awake now. Let's go." The Mortling moved its head, and shifted its eyes to her. She tried to look away, but found she couldn't. Voice strained she said, "Can it move? We need to keep going."

"Ya not understandin' what I be tryin' ta tell ya. Whatever give 'em the gift a' never bein' burdened by grief. It be gone! The Mortlins, they now takin' in every burden of sorrow they ever give ta the Tree, and it be like a disease eatin' at 'em from the inside. They got no way a' freein' they body, they mind, they heart from the pain and anguish of so many. All I done is give it a small relief, and my healin' ain't gonna last for long."

"What? No. Nothing you're saying makes sense. You said they'd help us. What does this have to do with Triste? I should never have come here."

Home, I need to be home. Triste will be fine. I'll find another doctor.

Veya's mother's voice, as clear as if she stood right next to her said, "This be your home and your Triste is here with ya right now."

Veya looked around half expecting to see her mother on the ledge where she stood, but Marie was not there.

I've lost my mind.

Brin looked at Veya, her eyes filled with tears. "Ya asked me 'bout the openin' and the stones 'round it? Why?" The Mortling had taken the stones off its body, and stood while helping Brin to stand as well. Brin's voice held an unusual heaviness, tears pooled in her eyes, "Ya been there? Mamma took ya there?"

Veya couldn't bare Brin's tears, or the idea of telling her the brief memory she'd just uncovered so she lied and said, "I don't know why I asked you that. No, I never went anywhere near this damn Tree. I've spent my entire life trying to rationalize the … the thing standing beside you. Mamma and her damn stones, taking sorrow. Well, maybe some people don't want their sorrow taken."

Brin wiped away the few tears she had let fall and smiled. Her forced upturned lips made Veya want to cry. She waited for her sister's argument, but none came. The Mortling had moved to where Veya assumed the steps going down from the ledge would be. Brin followed behind it.

Veya hesitantly looked to see if the white apparition still hovered over the green way stone. Her steps faltered; it was no longer there. In its place stood her daughter, her hand wrapped in the clawed fingers of a Hadling. Triste appeared as real as Brin, who had begun walking to the next step down.

Veya worried she might faint. She yelled, "Triste?"

Her daughter's name echoed back to her. The thing who she rationally knew could not be Triste did not respond. Instead it moved from the glow of the way stone. With the Hadling still holding its hand, they went down a step below the ledge, then another, and another, until they were beyond the stone's light. Moments later, they disappeared into the impenetrable void beyond Veya's reach, or vision.

Brin and the Mortling had reached the ledge where slimy, green roots rippled and slithered along the wall above the glowing stone. She motioned for Veya to follow, but Veya's eyes remained glued to the void where the Not-Triste had vanished. When she finally tore her eyes away, she could no longer see Brin or the Mortling.

She called to her sister, but received no answer. Her body didn't want to move another step. She wanted to lie down next to the sunny glowing stone and dream her way back to Ashland. But the green way stone was the first to be so close to the last. *Maybe now we'll have light all the way down.* She turned from the buttery warm glow and walked toward the grassy mirage where the Not-Triste had appeared.

Chapter Eleven

Veya trudged downward toward the green way stone. Her legs moved as though being sucked in by quicksand, while her vision again altered her reality. The steps seemed too many and wavered before her eyes. *Were there six to navigate or sixteen?* She felt trapped in a funhouse horror maze where a patch of grass appeared just below her, but remained always out of her reach.

No matter how hard she wished it, the Not-Triste didn't reappear.

Suddenly, the spell of the funhouse distortions was broken as Veya stepped onto a ledge larger than the last, bathed in a forest of green light.

Brin and the Mortling stood at the far end of the platform, their backs to her. Her sister was bent and whispering into the Mortling's ear. Bile caught in Veya's throat when Brin kissed the top of the creature's head before straightening.

Veya was weighed down with exhaustion, her mind a tangled web of disorientation. She worried she might run straight off the ledge and freefall into oblivion. She yearned for its release. She turned from Brin and the Mortling. She couldn't bear to hear any more about their mother, or the creatures, or the insanity of where they were, much less what they had to face next.

She anxiously tried to remember exactly where in the void she'd watched the apparition of her daughter vanish, and not for the first time wondered if her mind had finally been compromised. Could everything she was seeing, feeling, be an elaborate dream brought on by being on the Island once again? Walking inside a surreal Tree, being confined to the dark, knowing the beings her mother spoke of actually existed, it was all too much. She'd give anything to feel a breeze on her face, to see Triste picking wildflowers under a bright blue sky. From out of the nothingness where she stared, dazed, an illusion, as though summoned by her last thought of a teal blue sky, opened like the petals of a flower. She tried to enjoy the mirage her deranged mind created until it dawned on her the blue-green light wasn't a mirage.

The Not-Triste and the Hadling walked out of the haze cast by the way stone. They stood slightly below and straight across from her. The nervous stomach caused by her visual distortions visited her again. Everything morphed, not by some illusive mirror, but perhaps by the Tree itself? The ledge where they stood rippled with the brilliant teal glow of the way stone embedded at its center.

The Not-Triste's eyes stared directly at her. She'd never seen such anguish masked on her daughter's face. Not even in her deepest, darkest gray periods.

No, it's not my Triste. It's all a trick of my mind.

She tried to look away, but the tears falling down its cheeks, cheeks she knew held twin dimples when they were lifted by her smile, caught Veya, and held her there. It began walking backward while lifting its arms toward Veya, beckoning her to join it. Veya tore her gaze from the specter in search of the Hadling. The creature was nowhere to be seen. She scanned the area the stone's glow allowed.

She turned back to see the Not-Triste had stopped its backward movement.

Their eyes locked together again. Its jaw dropped down, its mouth hung open then moved as it spoke in jerks like a marionette puppet, maneuvered by strings. She strained to hear the words coming from within it.

"My stone Mamma, where—is—my—stone?" Its jaw snapped shut.

Triste's tortured voice tore through Veya.

No, impossible!

She looked down at the ledge and then to her right where the next set of steps would begin, if they followed the same pattern as those they'd already taken. She had to get to the next way stone. She had to know if the apparition was real. But where steps should've been, a wall of bark stood, blocking her way.

Where are they?

She turned in search of Brin. It began speaking again.

"Why—why—don't—I—have—a—stone—Mamma?" *Its* mouth lay open for a beat, then, locked shut once more. Its eyes held a questioning glare.

The force of each word sliced through Veya, causing her more agony than any real wound ever could.

The Not-Triste's eyes closed. When they opened again they'd returned to a stony stare. The body once again traveled backwards toward the Tree's wall and away from the outer edge of the shelf.

The pain of its words clung to Veya, and had barely subsided when a thunderous crash shook the platform under her feet, followed by a bone-chilling shriek.

What was that?

Another shriek came from the shadows, something being torn and ripped apart.

She frantically looked around for Brin. Her sister and the Mortling were no longer on the ledge with her.

"Brin? Where are you? Brin? What is that?"

She looked across to the Not-Triste. The way stone's greenish-blue color flickered, giving the Tree's bark behind the apparition the illusion of movement. But the movement wasn't an illusion. The bark on the Tree *was* moving, falling away, creating a small opening. She expected water to rush through, but when none came she held on to a moment of hope. *An escape?*

She barely noticed that the platform shook under her. Her focus remained on the undulating movement and outward bulge of the Tree's wall. The bark continued to split open wider and wider behind the still as a statue Not-Triste. All hope of escape vanished when through the large gap a hand with clawed, leathery fingers each the size of her torso emerged. The sharp talons sliced through the thick wood as though it were no more than mere water and reached toward the flowing gown of the Not-Triste. Farther and farther the hand came through the gaping hole, growing longer, giving the appearance of the Tree growing, not roots, but jagged deadly fingers.

The Not-Triste's eyes remained locked on Veya as it again began moving backward straight into the hand's beckoning grip.

"No, look out. Stop!" Veya stood suspended on the ledge's rim, high above the spectacle, unable to move. The toes of her galoshes again touched air; her heels rocked backward. She didn't want to witness the contorted fingers wrap around the gown with the sprinkle of embroidered flowers at its neck.

It will have nothing to capture. It's only an apparition.

She had to believe everything was an illusion formed by whatever created the insanity she'd been cast into. The tricks of her mind, the Tree, the creatures, perhaps all a ruse planned and carried out by the person she'd always blamed—her Mother.

But the hand did not grab air. Fingers the size of an adult human body seized a solid being wrapped in a soft white gown. Inch by inch, clutching tightly to a body unable to fight its grip, the hand withdrew back through the hole ripped in the Tree's wall. The body collapsed, limp, yet its arms still reached out toward Veya. In the time it took Veya to blink, the hand had dissolved back through the Tree. The ripped bark slowly closed around the beseeching arms until hands, palms up, were all that remained frozen in a sealed wall of bark. In the time it took Veya to blink again, they too, were absorbed until the Tree was once again a solid wall of bark.

The way stone's flickering light returned the illusion of gentle movement along the Tree's bark wall as though none of what Veya witnessed had ever occurred.

Triste?

On weak legs Veya backed away from the rim. Light-headed and drained, she tried desperately to comprehend what she'd seen. Behind her, the green way stone's glow revealed liquid seeping between the tuberous roots growing along the Tree's wall.

Water?

She placed her hand against the bark; the liquid, hot and thick, felt more like mucus than water.

Sap?

She tried forcing her hand through the bark where the fluid dripped, hoping the bark would be spongy, allowing her hand to easily slide through. It would be a logical explanation for what she'd just seen, even if she couldn't reason away the massive clawed hand. But no matter how much she tried, her hand could not penetrate the unyielding bark of the Tree.

There is no reality here. I'm in a dream. It wasn't her, my Triste. It's a nightmare taking control of my mind.

Yet, when she turned from the wall, Brin stood solidly beside her, hand in hand with the Mortling.

Veya directed her sister's gaze down to where milky white hands had been sucked into the Tree. Pointing toward the glowing empty teal tinged ledge she said, "Did you see? Did you see that?"

Did I see it?

Her sister didn't respond. Veya followed Brin's gaze to the exact spot where Veya had earlier searched for a way off the ledge. She shook her head in disbelief at the indention of a step following the spiral pattern they'd been walking down.

She yelled at Brin, "But the steps weren't there! Tree bark blocked my way." Yet, there they were, carved from the Tree's bark just as all the rest had been.

Brin had not responded to Veya's question. Instead she stood with her lips moving, but no sound came from them. Her eyes darted back and forth as they had done when she'd been "speaking" to their mamma. The Mortling pulled at Brin's hand, leading her away and toward the step down.

Veya stood momentarily paralyzed, then managed to whisper, "Brin? Please don't leave me." A moment later her shaking legs collapsed and she landed hard on the stone platform, her body an empty shell.

She sat crossed legged, her shoulders slumped, her face cradled in her hands, and closed her eyes. Instinctually she began massaging the closed lids with her index and middle finger.

Calm down. Breathe.

She opened her eyes and gazed past the green ledge and out to the wavering light of the teal blue way stone to see if her sister had reached it yet. The ledge was empty. An all too familiar wave of panic pulled at her chest.

Stop it! You won't take me.

She could at least control her own body, if nothing else around her. She focused on her breathing; the anxiety eased.

What am I doing?

Her eyes remained on the empty ledge. The wavering green-blue light reminded her of the ocean waves along the Oregon coast she and Triste visited every summer. So open, so calming, so serene. So not like the claustrophobic, dense overgrowth that blocked her view of the sky on the Island.

She massaged her eyelids again. The circular motion created the desired soothing affect she'd been taught by the first of her many mediation gurus. But the effect was fleeting. A stark cold sizzled through every nerve in her sweat-drenched body, as the absurdity of attempting to meditate while she questioned her own sanity struck her. No meditation, no amount of therapy—nothing—nothing she'd done had ever really made *any* of what she'd attempted to forget, to bury, go away. Not the few memories she recalled of her traumatic childhood, not her abandonment issues surrounding her mother, not her dead grandmamma, not even the cruel laughter of Triste's father. He'd laughed at her when, in her youthful innocence, she'd happily told him of the baby they'd created. Hadn't his uncaring laughter followed her through every relationship she'd had since? All of it, no matter how hard she'd tried, all of it still clung to her.

With her eyes still closed and gripped in the turmoil of her sudden realization, something moved behind her.

"What ya be doin'?" Brin was back. "Triste said ya need ta find her stone. So, if I be you, I be gettin' up and goin' on down ta the heart center. Ya ain't gonna find nothin' but more pain by sittin' here."

"But I don't … I can't, I can't move. I can't do this … it's all so … so insane."

"Ya can't or ya won't? Mamma said ya always took the easy way out. It be why ya had no bother over leavin' us, or her, ta take on what needed done."

"What, me leaving? That didn't cause Mamma anything. I actually relieved her by giving her more time to spend being the famous Sorrow Keeper of the Island. She lives for her followers, her flock worshipping her. Them, and you."

"Ya be wrong. She grieved hard when ya left."

"Right. I suppose it's why neither she nor our father ever once tried to visit me after I told you where I lived. Did they even ask if you knew?"

"Ya got no knowin' on how things be."

Veya had her answer. They'd never asked.

She didn't intend to raise her voice, but she did when she said, "Stop. You're the one with no knowing. You, her happy bundle of joy, you don't know. I had to beg her, beg my own mother, to attend the awards ceremony when I received my college scholarship. Do you have any idea how hard I worked to get that? She never once attended any of the school functions other mothers did. Why? Some of my classmates thought her either dead or insane given the rumors of what she did." Veya stood, inches from Brin's face. "Don't ever tell me again about Mamma and her sacrifices, because it's you who doesn't know."

Unfazed Brin said, "So ya goin' back. Ya gonna just leave her here. I seen her beggin' ya to help her."

"So, you did see *it*? I suppose you have some explanation? What the hell is the, the thing that looks like my daughter? And the hand that came out of the Tree, what was it? Does the Tree actually give birth to the creatures? What is this place, really?" She waved her arms to encompass everything around her, waiting for an answer.

"It ain't only a Tree. It be the Hadlins' and Mortlins' home. Always been they home, always will be they home." Brin's eyes, etched by creases Veya had not noticed, looked down at the Mortling. The thin line of her lips turned up slightly as though reassuring it. Brin moved toward the step to go down.

"Wait, why won't you answer me? What is the phantom thing with Triste's face? I refuse to believe it is any part of my daughter."

"It be your child all right. It be everythin' she is, 'cept the thing what houses it. It be all her thoughts, all her rememberin', all her seein' and tastin'. It be everythin', but her blood-flowing body. That be what lay dyin' in the hospital, and if'n we don't get her and her stone from the Hadlins, she be trapped here in this place. Her body be the only thing that'll die. But *she*, what the preachers call her soul, it be still livin' on, here. She be forever entombed in the Tree."

"How is that possible?"

"I don't got a knowin' I can give ya in words 'bout such things, the hows or whys. It be a knowin' born ta me in my bones. The Mortlins and Hadlins, they been here a mighty long time. We got little knowin' 'bout the whys a' them too, just some words writ by past Keepers in a book. But I be believin' Mamma when she says your Triste be a part a' fixin' what ain't right with 'em no more. I done told ya the Mortlins be dyin' and maybe the Hadlins be dyin' too. I'm thinkin' the next way stone can't be far past that there blue-green one."

Having said all she had to say, Brin turned from Veya and followed the Mortling down the ever-spiraling path. The fluid dripping from the Tree pooled in spots on the crude steps.

Veya followed and wished for the umpteenth time she had on her hiking boots with their thick tread instead of the slick goulashes. The boots sat in her hallway closet in Ashland. Her cottage home in Ashland with its cozy covered front porch seemed another lifetime ago. It appeared in her mind's eye side by side with that of her family's home on the Island. The homes were identical other than the Island home's screened-in front porch. No screen was necessary to keep out the mosquitos in Ashland. She paid close attention to the sticky sludge coming from the Tree, watching her step, while trying to divine the meaning of the similarity in the homes. How many more things had followed her from the Island to her new life in Ashland?

When she reached the ledge where the teal way stone glowed, she stopped long enough to run her hands over the area where she'd seen the clawed hand rip through the Tree. No evidence remained of the bark being disturbed, or of a body clad in white.

The madness of it all caught her for a moment, before a stronger intuition took over. She turned from the way stone and continued her descent. The liquid flowing from the walls of the Tree had increased. With each step she expected her foot to be submerged in water. But even though the liquid, giving off a metallic scent, dripped heavily it never pooled too deep. The light above her faded. With only the glow of her necklace, she willingly walked toward the impenetrable darkness yet again.

"Brin?" she called out.

"I be on another ledge, but there be no way stone lightin' it. Stay put till I see what's a'coverin' it. Must be what been drippin' all 'round me."

Veya counted each inhale and exhale of her breath. Ten. Then moved down onto the next step. No way was she going to stay still. Her foot hit the solid protrusion, and it slid from under her. Grabbing at an indentation in the Tree's bark she leaned into the Tree to stabilize herself. While she hugged the Tree the flowing thick, warm liquid coated her hand and crept up her arm.

Brin's voice echoed from below, "I got it."

A deep blue lit up the puddle at Veya's feet.

"What is this stuff, sap?" she asked, needing to hear another human voice while inching her way down to a sitting position. She scooted to the next niche. The liquid flowed in erratic intervals; the next step was dry. Her worry of water gushing in when the Tree had been torn open by the clawed hand came back. She now wondered if the liquid was the bayou seeping through the Tree.

What if it breaks through?

"Brin, did you hear me? What's this stuff coming out of the tree? Brin?"

She wiped the slime from her arms, and stepped onto the ledge where the next cobalt blue way stone cast its light. Her sister stood directly over the stone staring straight ahead, inches from the Tree's wall. Brin had pulled the hood of her slicker over her head. For once the Mortling wasn't at Brin's side. Its trembling body stood dangerously close to the ledge's rim. The stone's light cast onto the red of Brin's slicker, gave the effect of a halo above her head. The image reminded Veya of the Virgin Mary painting hanging above the mantle in their mother's bedroom.

Veya studied the Mortling. Something wasn't right. She looked back at her sister. Brin's eyes were open wide, filled with a fear Veya had never once seen in her sibling. Their twin stones swayed on their necks casting an ominous shadow on Brin's face. In a trembling voice Brin said, "Dear God in Heaven, what's goin' on?"

When Veya saw what Brin had been staring at, her body propelled her back so fast, if not for someone catching her once again, she'd have fallen right off the ledge. This time it was the Mortling who caught her. Her momentary confusion over the creature saving her life vanished when she looked toward what had caused her alarm. Submerged in the bark of the tree were pieces and parts of bodies, horned ears, hanging flesh, claws, leathery fingers, tails—the bodies of Mortlings and Hadlings. Looking closely she reassured herself there were no human appendages. The thick liquid dripped from what she assumed were lifeless limbs.

Until, a clawed finger moved.

And, an eye opened.

It's not real!

Brin's voice, laden with terror yelled, "We got ta get out a' here. Now!" She grabbed the Mortling's hand and jumped from the ledge.

What the hell? Had Brin just jumped into thin air?

A dizzying seesaw of panic swept over Veya when she heard movement below. She pulled at the small stone around her neck to cast as much light as possible and peered over the edge of the shelf. "Are you okay?" She heard what she hoped was Brin's movement, but she couldn't see her. She inched carefully to step off the ledge, anxious to escape the grisly sight of the deep blue glow dancing against encased appendages.

Brin yelled, "It's the Tree, Veya. Not the Hadlins. It's the Tree what be after us. It be dyin', and it be my fault. I don't know why, but the Tree be tryin' ta trap your Triste, me, you, the Hadlins and Mortlins. We all goin' ta die inside a' it."

Chapter Twelve

Veya fought to understand Brin's words.

The Tree?

The instant the words penetrated, Veya remembered the Telling Card with the image of a body being wrapped, held upside down. The exact same image she'd witnessed of her sister encased, mummified in the Tree's branches. The memory of the sensation she'd had when branches tightened around her body paralyzed her from leaving the ledge. In her pocket, the weight of the stones warmed against her thigh.

The Tree, the opening, the andirons, you have to remember. No, I don't want to. Her mind battled with her anxiety and dread.

She stood frozen in the blue glow, unable to pull her eyes from the grim sight embedded in the Tree.

An arm twitched.

A head jerked.

Then seemingly petrified hands uncurled their fingers from stationary fists. Two hands moved, extending their fingers out by slicing through the Tree just as the monstrous clawed hand had. They were escaping their captivity as though the bark again had no more substance than warmed butter. The arms attached to the hands followed. In the time it took Veya to move to the edge of the shelf and step down, the entire body of a Hadling had pulled itself from within the wall of the tree.

It lurched forward, arms extended in an attempt to capture her.

Veya tried desperately to unravel the words Brin had yelled. Images of the Tree ran through her mind: over-large hands pulling the Not-Triste inside the Tree's walled bark, the Tree's limbs lifting her and Brin off the bridge, Tree roots engulfing the Village. She wondered again if the Tree actually birthed the creatures, but she couldn't reason her way beyond the scream echoing through her brain.

The Tree! Dear God how am I supposed to escape a Tree?

When the Hadling came within inches of her, she ran with a heightened sense of the sounds behind her. The hollowed-out niches that formed the steps were now closer together and less inclined. In order to see if the Hadling followed, she got on all fours and began crawling backward down. To her surprise she found she moved much faster.

We must be near the base of the Tree. But then what? Will the Tree absorb us all?

"Brinnn?" Desperation echoed in circles above and below.

Her notion of seeing if the Hadling followed was flawed. She had no idea, because the blue light had faded in the distance. The meager light from her necklace remained her only defense against her tomb of darkness. At the slightest sound she startled, and lay flat against the niches hoping to be unseen. The liquid coming from the tree had not yet reached the lower level. She wouldn't allow for the notion that the occasional scrape or scuff below her was anything other than Brin. When her foot caught on something lying in the recess of a step's niche, she pulled out the offending item, her sister's rain slicker. Brin's pouch of stones fell from its pocket. She picked up the pouch, placed it back in the pocket, and tied the jacket over her own rain slicker at her waist.

Did it come untied when she jumped?

"Brin!" No answer.

Veya's stomach tightened. Her foot searched for the next step. Finding it, she stood and continued down. The fear of being left alone overcame the terror of giving away her location. She yelled again, "Brin, damn it, answer me! Where are you?"

Below and to the right a faint lavender pinpoint of light penetrated the midnight black of her existence. A shadow came into view. Given the miniature stature, she assumed it to be a Mortling. It stood alone, no taller figure near. The closer the spiraling steps took Veya toward the scene unfolding before her, the closer dread stalked in her wake. She'd witnessed the scene before, only in the previous scene Brin had been standing on the way stone's ledge and the Mortling had lain flat and unmoving. In this scene, the Mortling stood over her sister's motionless body.

When Veya reached the ledge, Brin's face was turned from her, yet she heard her say, "What took ya so long?"

She's alive.

Veya shoved the Mortling aside, her hand making contact with its body. She couldn't pull away from the warm, moist leathery skin fast enough. Deafening words reverberated through her mind. "Welcome, home, Veya. Welcome, we knew you'd come."

Unsettled, her hand numb, she looked around to see if someone or something else shared the ledge with them. *Is it the Mortling talking to me?* She wiped the glistening moisture of its skin from her hand, rubbing hard against her jeans' rough fabric. Her hand gleamed.

Scales? Is it covered in scales?

Her sister moaned. The words placed in her mind faded to a faint whisper, embedded, an unwanted mantra.

Welcome home. We knew you'd come.

She turned her attention to Brin. "What happened? Why did you jump?"

Brin's unblinking eyes stared up at her.

"What … the … hell?" Veya stuttered. The face surrounding Brin's eyes wasn't her sister's face. Its eyes were her sister's smiling blue eyes, and Brin's long red flames of hair framed the face. But the face, the face, etched in fine spidery lines of age, was not her sister's youthful rosy skin.

Veya quickly looked away from Brin, then back again, unsure of what she was seeing. She tried to hide the concern she was certain showed on her own face.

Brin lifted her hand to her face as though trying to feel what Veya saw while saying, "Calm down Veya. I be fine. Takes some out a' me ta do what need doin'. The Mortlins, the Hadlins, and maybe even the Tree be needin' my help. I must'a dropped my coat in my hurry. Did ya come upon it on it on your way down? I been a lookin' for it. I be needin' my bag a' healin' Stones."

"I don't understand. What do you mean *help*? Yes, I found these." Veya pulled out her sister's red bag, and untied the enclosure. She started to pour the stones in her own hand.

"No, don't." Brin reached out and caught the stones as they fell from the bag. "There be too much grief in these here stones for even you ta take." Brin poured the stones back in the bag, tied and shut it, then tucked the pouch in the cleavage of her blouse.

"What do you mean for even *me*? What's happened to you?" The words were barely spoken, when the Hadling she thought had not followed her stepped onto the ledge. The creature's slow, jerky, movements cast erratic violet colored shadows onto the ledge. The Hadling moved toward Brin, its clawed hand clung to its chest. The bird's skull hanging from its neck no longer showed a glowing ember.

Veya stood to face the Hadling. "What do I do? How do I stop it?"

Brin got up, but Veya could see it took some effort. Once standing, Brin said in a commanding voice, "Move out of the way, Veya." Veya moved. Her sister's slow gait mimicked that of the Hadling. Brin walked to the Mortling, and began dropping the stones from her bag into its hand.

Expecting at any moment to see yet another Hadling come from within the Tree, Veya moved away from the Tree's wall.

The Mortling reached its hand filled with stones toward the Hadling. The Hadling, still clutching at its chest, didn't move. Something slithered near the Hadling's feet. Veya looked more closely. The something wasn't a thing. It was the Hadling's rat-like feet growing longer, and longer. As they grew they morphed from their leathery sinew to barked tree roots.

Veya blinked, not trusting what she was seeing. But when she opened her eyes, the feet-roots were snaking along the ledge and surrounding the purple way stone.

Panic burst from Veya. "What the hell is that?"

Brin didn't respond. Her eyes were focused on the Hadling.

Veya's gaze warily shifted back to the Hadling who had removed its hand from its chest. In the very spot it had clutched, a small oblong hole the size of a quarter appeared.

I've seen this before.

The hole expanded until the creature's chest lay splayed open about a foot long. The gap ran vertically from the flap of hanging flesh at the base of its face to the middle of its torso.

No! This isn't real. Wake up. Wake up.

Inside the cavity of its chest, the same viscous liquid flowing from the Tree coated a web of forest green, pulsing, thin gnarled tubers the size of its claw. The tubers looked exactly like the roots winding and crawling along the wall of the tree. The violet crystalline way stone began pulsing to the same rhythm as the viscera in the Hadling's chest.

The Mortling with its hand still outstretched, moved toward the Hadling.

Close your eyes.

But her eyes would not close.

She had to see.

She had to remember.

As though they were heating up, a foggy mist formed around the nest of stones the Mortling held. From the mist came a ribbon of smoky-gray twisting tendrils. The tendrils drifted toward the Hadling's open chest, winding around the pulsating flesh until they were absorbed by it.

No, I don't want to see this again. It was just a foolish child's dream!

Everything around Veya spun. She was trapped in a vortex of fear while familiar panic cascaded through her.

Tearing her eyes away from the scene, her mind chanted, *This isn't happening. Swamp rats, they were swamp rats. They were swamp rats …*

When she looked again the mist had begun to dissipate. The opening in the Hadling's chest slowly closed until there was no evidence it had existed at all.

The Mortling poured the stones back in Brin's hand. Then it, and the Hadling, whose feet were no longer rooted to the Tree's shelf, walked to the edge and stood facing the sisters. The two creatures left a space between them as though inviting the women to walk through the opening.

Brin extended the hand holding the stones to Veya. "Ya can hold 'em now. The Hadlin' done ate most a' the sorrow from 'em. What left be given ta the Tree."

"Ate?" Veya couldn't finish the question. Her whole body shivered.

Brin slumped against Veya's trembling body.

Veya eased herself and her sister down to the ground. They sat crossed legged, knees touching. Pressure built inside of Veya's head. She feared her psyche would shatter at any moment, leaving her an empty shell—a corpse perpetually living in the hell around her—forever searching for Triste.

Brin's strained smile beamed over at Veya. Fine lines cascaded around the dimples Veya had forgotten her sister possessed. Dimples, identical to Triste's.

Brin took Veya's hands in her own and held them. Veya didn't often touch her patients, but when the occasion necessitated, she used the same comforting gesture. It was a therapeutic technique used to get the patient to break through a particular mental barrier.

Her sister's face unnerved Veya. She looked away and up at the creatures. They stood as though stationary statues on either side of an unknown entrance, waiting for someone or something to pass through.

Without warning, a lightning bolt of pain shot through Veya's head, and her vision immediately tunneled down to the small area where the creatures stood. She waited for her chest to tighten. It didn't. It wasn't panic.

I've seen them like this before.

The déjà vu of a Mortling and Hadling standing at an entrance, each with their hands resting on an andiron coursed through her body, an electrical current.

Brin's hands squeezed hers. Her voice came to Veya from a long distance away. "I done figured all a' this out, Veya. Now ya gots ta remember. Your Triste be a'waitin' on ya."

The memory of the andirons abducted Veya. It sparked from the base of her spine and up the back of her head before shattering. Along the edges of her vision, glittering flashes floated. She was no longer with Brin. She was no longer a thirty-nine-year-old woman. She was the ten-year-old girl who had long ago buried a memory. The memory of doing something her mamma had forbid her from ever doing.

As Veya sat with her sister's hands clinging to her own, the memory played in her mind; a grainy, black and white film.

Before dawn that day, she'd followed her mamma when she'd left the house. She figured it'd be like playin' hide and seek only she was doin' the hidin' and she hoped her mamma wouldn't be seekin' her. She wanted to know where her mamma went all the time. When her mamma got to where she was going, the rats was a standin' waitin' on either side of a monster Tree. The Tree's mouth was open. It was dark inside. It swallowed her mamma and the rats whole. She didn't want to follow her mamma and be eaten by the Tree, but she had to know if what the other kids said 'bout her mamma bein' a devil worshiper was true. She let the Tree eat her too. Inside a' the Tree there was shiny stones everywhere.

Tears welled in Veya's eyes. She opened them and looked directly at her sister's own tear-glistening eyes. "I don't want to do this," she whispered.

Brin's smile barely reached her lips. "We all gots stones ta carry, and stones ta bury. What come 'afore gonna come again, till the burden we carry done get eaten, and buried."

Brin's voice swirled around Veya in a hypnotic chant. "Stones ta carry, and stones ta bury."

Veya returned to the memory.

She crouched in a corner of the Tree. Her mamma stood next to a big rock table. The rats was standin' on top a' it. One a 'em's innards was a showin'. They was stones, and small animal bones, everywhere she looked. She stepped over the bones. Her stomach was a flowin' in ta her throat. But she couldn't let any noise come out, or her mamma would hear her. The rat cut a openin' in its chest with its big claw. Its innards was movin' like snakes buried in a nest. She tried to hold the scream in, but it escaped out a' her right 'afore everythin' round her was sucked in ta a tiny black hole. All the shiny stones' lights went out. When her mamma's scary eyes found her she tried to run back through the Tree's mouth, but her mamma caught the back a her shirt. "No, Mamma please let me go, please. I didn't see nothin' I promise. Please let me go."

Her mamma's voice commanded from the darkness, "I be lettin' the Mortlin' tell me if I need let ya go."

Veya pulled herself back to the present and tried to explain to Brin what she'd allowed herself to remember. "I'd never heard the thing's name, *Mortling*, until I followed Mamma to the Tree. It was a ten-year old girl's stupid prank. When Mamma caught me, she allowed the creature to touch me, look at me, breathe on me. It's taken me years to keep the horror of that day buried and forgotten. How could she allow such a thing? I was a child, a child! We need to finish this now." She tried to stand, but Brin held her down.

"I be needin' ta know what happened after the Mortlin' touched ya." Brin let tears fall freely from her eyes, not bothering to wipe them from her face.

"No, I'm done. I can't, don't you see, I can't." Even as she said the words, something fought from deep inside of her, something ripping and tearing its way out.

Dear God, what's happening to me?

Brin's soft voice penetrated Veya's paralyzing terror. "All I ever wanted in this here life was ta be a Sorrow Keeper, takin' away people's pain and sufferin'. I wanted ta be a mamma too. Bet ya didn't know that? Dr. Mary says it ain't ta be."

Veya tried to pull herself back to comfort her sister, but Brin continued her lyrical chant. "Stones ta carry, and stones ta bury. Ya been hurtin' a mighty long time. Ain't ya ready to let go a' such a burden?"

The thing battling to escape from Veya propelled her over an invisible ledge, and through the mental barricades of her long-buried memories.

She was ten years old again, and lying on a rock table. The rats put stones on her chest over her dress. The stones were so hot she worried they'd burn right through her. Her mamma stood next ta her with wide-open eyes, but there was no seein' in 'em. Her mamma whispered words over and over. When her mamma's eyes come back ta livin', she looked down at Veya and said, "The lineage will remain … Keeper you shall …"

Veya pulled herself back from the abyss of the memory yelling, "No more!"

She tried to move away from Brin, but her body shook so uncontrollably all she could manage was pulling her hands from Brin's. When she'd calmed, she said, "I jumped from the table and ran. I had no idea what pressed down on my chest, why I couldn't breathe. It was my first panic attack. I either passed out or fell somewhere along the path outside the Tree. Daddy found me, and took me home. Our mother hadn't even bothered to come after me, or to look for me. I ran, because I didn't want to hear what she was going to say. But I know, I guess I've always known, and now so do you. She and I never spoke about it, and she allowed me to believe everything I remembered from that day was caused by seeing a swamp rat, followed by tripping and hitting my head." Pointing to the Hadling and Mortling she continued, "Now do you see? Do you see why she's as much a monster to me as they are?"

Veya pulled away when Brin tried to hold her hands again. Any small amount of energy she still possessed drained from her. She whispered, "I am no Sorrow Keeper. I've never wanted to be the Keeper. Never!"

"It was always supposed ta be ya, Veya. It must'a been what Mamma meant when she said she'd done everythin' for ya. She tried ta get 'em to take me instead. I understand now why they didn't. If I got no seeds, no baby ta carry on the line a' Keepers, well they wasn't ever gonna take me. Now 'cause a' what Mamma done it's all wrong, and I don't know if'n we can fix it. But I do know it's you they be wantin', and your Triste is caught up in what needs fixin'. They'll keep her till we sort through our wrong doin'. First ya gotta accept your place as they Keeper. Then we'll see if it be enough ta get your Triste and Mamma back."

Veya stood. She had to move, to get away. She crept to the opening where the creatures were and yelled at them. "Take *her!*" She pointed to Brin. "She wants this. I do not!" The creatures didn't move or acknowledge in any way they understood what she'd said.

Veya walked between them and looked down over the edge of the shelf. They'd reached the Tree's heart center.

The final spiral of steps descended and ended at the last gleaming brilliant white way stone. Its beam cast an eerie glow onto the rock table. The same table she'd remembered her ten-year-old body lying on. The thick liquid flowing from the Tree swirled in pools around the base of the table. On top of the table's ebony stone surface a white gown gleamed. The garment had been placed perfectly, laid out as though waiting for its mistress to lift it over her head before a restful night's slumber. Veya didn't have to see them to know embroidered flowers were at its neck. Surrounding the table were dozens of Hadlings and Mortlings.

Chapter Thirteen

Veya walked to Brin and helped her lift her frail body. Once Brin was up Veya asked, "What have they done with Triste, or whatever the thing is that looks like her? I'm done with half answers and half truths." She hated the horror-filled edge in her voice, and the distress etched on her sister's face did nothing to alleviate its stifling presence. But she continued her inquisition. "We came to get Mamma and Triste's stones back. How do we do that?" Her words came out in a hoarse strangle. Her parched throat begged for the last few sips from her water bottle, while her stomach protested its need for food.

Brin leaned heavily on Veya and said, "I wish I had the answers you be needin'. All I know is we got ta get down there. Ya gonna have ta help me. I be needin' everythin' I got ta give ta the Mortlins if the time comes."

Veya didn't care to know what the Mortlings might need from her sister. The white nightgown spread upon the altar spurred her on.

She wondered if Brin could feel her shaking as they stood side by side. She asked again, "Do you have any idea what's going to happen down there?"

They were facing out toward the center of the Tree, and even though she couldn't see over the ledge to where the creatures were, she knew they were still there—waiting. Her mind tried in vain to grasp what might be required of her when they made their way to the final way stone—to the heart center. She needed to know. She had to be prepared.

Brin didn't answer. Instead she reached over and cupped her warm, soft hands around Veya's cheeks. Veya clasped her own shaking hands together. They were cold and clammy. The sisters stood in silence, disturbed only by the occasional drip of water, or the click of a Hadling's claw. The longer they stood, eyes locked, the more the crawling terror wrapped around Veya eased.

Is Brin doing this? Veya startled with the realization of the power emanating from her sister's hands.

Questions, so many questions wanted to come forth. But something in Veya had shifted since her recovered memory, and she knew if she started to speak, if the words came out, so would the bayou of tears she'd been holding in check.

What is she doing to me?

She allowed the silence, and solace coming from Brin's touch to cocoon her from her own thoughts and feelings.

How long could they remain alone, locking out everything, everyone else?

No! We need to finish this!

She tried to pull Brin's hands from her face, but her sister's lips turned up into a brilliant smile, stopping Veya from her task. For that brief moment, Brin turned back into Veya's sunny, happy, dimple-faced baby sister. It was for one beat of Veya's heart, but the dazzling smile threatened to open another chasm of the dark waters she'd held so dear for so very long. The weight of the emotion was more than she could bear. She ripped Brin's hands from her face, and when she looked at Brin again, her sister was no longer youthful, but had returned to a fragile, aged woman.

With arms wrapped around each other's waists they began their descent down the last curve of the spiral stairs. Below them the final silvery white way stone cast flickering sparks within the shadows of the deep, dark niches filled with the unknown. A few steps beyond the way stone lay the Tree's heart center, and the altar so recently chiseled from Veya's memories.

"What are we going to do when we get there? Am I going to have to lie on that damn table again? Am I the sacrifice to bring Triste back?" The snake of dread was back, but not at the base of her head any longer. It had slithered from her torso like a reptile and now curled heavy in the pit of her stomach.

Brin moved her hand from around Veya's waist and placed it under the collar of her sister's blouse, resting it on her shoulder blade, skin to skin. Once again the phenomenon of her sister's touch uncoiled the nest of apprehension growing ever stronger within her. Her sister's breath warm on her ear, whispered, "It's gonna be okay. I'll see ta it. Now let's get down there. I expect they been a'waitin' on us a mighty long time." A rose scent filled Veya's senses. *Grandmamma?* They walked toward the table. The Mortlings and Hadlings parted as they went.

When they reached the raised slab of rock, Veya stopped and stood on the balls of her feet so she could see the top where the white gown had been.

The gown was no longer there.

They stepped to the center in the light of the shimmering way stone. The weight of her sister's hand still rested on her shoulder. She didn't turn to face Brin. Instead she asked in a murmur, "What's next?" Focused on the glowing crystalized stone she waited for her sister's response while keeping her head down, knowing there were many eyes peering at them. Some from out of dark corners.

When Brin didn't answer she twisted her head around to see if her sister was okay. Brin's eyes were closed once again, her lips moving; no sound came from them.

Is she talking to them, or is Mamma talking to her, telling her what to do?

A surge of anger rose inside Veya at the thought of their controlling mother. She reached up, and slapped Brin's face. Shock at what she'd done coursed through her, but still her sister would not speak, or open her eyes.

Maybe, she's praying? Praying?

She had no idea where the thought of praying came from. She'd never been exposed to a spiritual belief system. At least not any belief other than the jumble of superstitious rituals of their mother. Veya's faith had been placed solidly in knowledge. Tangible things she could touch and see. Yet as she struggled to comprehend, to make any rational sense of her current predicament, the irony of how little use her resolute logic was struck her like fire-fueled fingers running along every nerve in her body. Her knees buckled and she fought to remain standing, while her exhausted mind tried frantically to hold on to its waning sanity.

The Mortling and Hadling who'd been on the ledge with them at the lavender way stone had followed them down to the heart center. The Mortling stood beside Brin, the Hadling beside Veya. A current of alarm flowed up and down Veya's spine.

What if Brin stays in this trance?

Veya waited. She continued to avoid looking out at the Mortlings and Hadlings standing or sitting in every nook and cranny where the stone cast its glow. Instead she concentrated on the liquid she'd seen from the ledge above. It flowed over and around hundreds of stones embedded in the Tree roots coiled along the ground where the table stood. Their color mimicked the stones she'd seen fixed in the Tree's bark before they'd begun walking across the bridge. Some were a distinct color, some smooth, some jagged cut, some simple river stones. Others were crystalized as all the way stones had been. All were set in a spiral design. The liquid flowing over and around them, along with the sparkling glow of the white way stone, gave them the illusion of movement. She stood mesmerized by their swirling motion. Each twisting coil resembled a galaxy crafted by stones.

How can this beauty exist in such horror?

She turned her focus from the twirling galaxies to look up at the table standing several feet away. The platform's pedestal was formed by Tree roots so large they could've been trees themselves. She estimated the ebony stone altar, a few inches taller than her, to be about six feet wide and twice as long. The light cast upon it by the silvery way stone gave the platform a shimmering element. Embedded in the rooted base were stones of the same spiraling pattern as those with water flowing over them. Still more stones glinted along the rough-cut edges of the altar.

"Brin? You still with me?" She tried to turn to see her sister. Brin, with a strength she'd not possessed before, had placed both her hands firmly on Veya's shoulders, holding her in place, facing forward.

"Yes, I be here now." Brin's breath heated the back of Veya's neck, and her voice increased from a faint whisper to a booming cry echoing through the cavern of the Tree, "Veya, where be your stones?"

Veya tried to break free from her sister's grip, but the movement caused Brin's fingers to dig deeper into her shoulders.

"What do you mean my stones? I don't have any stones. Just this." Her fingers wrapped around the amulet hanging from her neck. "You're hurting me. Let loose. What are you doing?"

Again Brin's forceful voice, "Where are your stones, your many stones?"

The pouch of stones Veya had placed in the pocket of her jeans weighed heavy against her leg.

Veya pulled out the velour white bag . "You mean these? These aren't mine. These are the stones Mamma sent to Triste."

"Take the stones out a' the bag, Veya. Hold 'em in your hand. Now."

"I ..." Confusion clouded Veya's words. "I don't understand."

Brin's voice softened, "Please." She released her firm grip on Veya's shoulders.

Veya's unsteady fingers untied the knot from the pouch. She let the stones fall to her open palm one by one.

The way stone's sparking glow made each shimmer in midair before they hit her heat-moistened skin.

As each one hit her palm the snake of dread coiled in the pit of her stomach shot up her spine again and again, like molten lava igniting at the back of her skull. With the final stone released from the bag, the snake carrying all its emotion sprang, exploding so intensely, she had to stifle a scream. Brin gripped her shoulders, again holding her in a vice-like grip.

"Whose stones are they, Veya?"

"Brin, I don't know what you're talking about." She lifted a garnet stone from her palm. The crimson rock was etched in a unique jagged cut, a rose opening its petals. Veya's voice started in a whisper and ended in a scream. "This looks like … No! It can't be!"

She tried to twist free, to see in her sister's eyes, but Brin would not let her turn. "I threw this stone away. I didn't keep it. Where did this come from?"

Another flick of heat at the back of her skull and through a flash of searing pain yet another memory emerged.

Veya stood on the front porch of their home with her mamma. Her grandmamma lay in an open coffin in their living room a few feet from where they stood. Islanders streamed in and out of the home paying their respects. Her mamma spoke, "Here child, take this here red stone. See how the cut make the tiny stone look like your grandmamma's favorite flower, a rose? The stone be bloomin' too. Since you be the … well, since you be my daughter you gonna have ta give the stone ta the Tree yourself ta release the grief ya be sufferin' for your grand-mamma dyin'. "

Another flick at the base of Veya's skull flung her back to the present. Her vision blurred from the pain, or was it the memory? She stared unbelieving at the blood red stone appearing to open like a rose, nestled amongst the others she'd dropped from the open pouch.

Brin's murmured words were spoken inches from her ear, yet they seemed to come to Veya through a faraway tunnel. "It be the stone Mamma give ya ta get rid a' your grievin' for our grandmamma."

"But how? How could it possibly be? I never placed the stone. I never placed any she gave me. I threw this one in the swamp. So how?" Agony sliced through her when she picked up another stone, a gray river stone, its jagged edges the shape of a crescent moon exactly like the stone given to her when her baby brother died. The one she'd buried at the base of his grave.

"How the hell?"

This isn't happening.

Veya's chest tightened, her vision tunneled. The panic would finally win.

Brin remained standing behind Veya, firmly holding her in place. When Brin replied Veya could feel Brin's moist lips on her ear. "In one way or the other ya been a carryin' your stones a' sorrow all along, Veya. Now, Mamma done give 'em back ta ya, what ya gonna do with 'em?"

Veya struggled to break free of her sister's hold on her. "Is this what all this is about, me giving my stones to this damn Tree? Me giving my sorrow, me giving in to Mamma's crazy … No, I won't be their Keeper, and I won't be a part of this … this … ritual."

Veya squeezed the stones. She needed pain to wake from this dream. They cut through the palm of her hand. Pinpricks of blood formed and coated them.

"Look at 'em, Veya. Look at *your* stones. They be yours not Triste's. Mamma's been a'keepin' 'em for ya. The stone she picked special for the grief ya took on after Triste be born be in there. Ya had no one ta ask when ya needed help. Look at 'em. All the stones ya been a carryin' 'round."

Veya kept her fist clenched.

"Okay, if'n you won't look at your stones, then look at *them*." Brin released her grip on Veya's shoulders, but quickly placed her hands once again on Veya's face, this time forcing her to look out at the creatures both obvious, and hidden in the shadows.

"They be dyin'. This here Tree be dyin' and all this be my fault, our fault, your fault, Mamma's fault. I wanted so bad, so bad to be they Keeper. Mamma, she was a tryin' ta give us, her daughters, both what we wanted. "

Veya finally looked up at the Mortlings and Hadlings. There was something not right. Some held on to one another for support in standing, while others slumped over, clutching at their chests. Still others tried to prod back to life those who lay curled in fetal positions. She closed her eyes against the harsh reality of what Brin said. They weren't her problem. She didn't care about them. She came for Triste, and as though bidden, when she opened her eyes the apparition of Triste, the Not-Triste, sat far off amongst the Hadlings and Mortlings. She no longer wore the white flowing gown sprinkled with embroidered flowers at its neck. Instead she wore the blood red robe of a Keeper, and at her waist, identical to Veya's mother's, a lavender pouch dangled.

"No!" Panic lashed around Veya's chest. Invisible ropes squeezed.

Triste—is—not—a Keeper!

The stones pulsed in her hand as she fought a rising tide of strangling terror. Along with the weight of her uncovered memories came the undeniable truth of the role she'd played in her own illusions.

Chapter Fourteen

Veya could not, would not, accept fault in Triste's illness. There had to be another explanation. It was her mother's doing, always her mother's doing. With the stones still beating in her hand she grabbed Brin's arm, demanding, "Where's Triste's stone? I have to give her protection. It's me they want, me, not her. Where is it?"

Brin jerked free from Veya, saying, "I got no answers for ya. The link be broken, and like I done said, I got a knowin' it be our doin', you, me, and Mamma. The circle what be in place since they beginnin', the bindin' between a Keeper, a Mortlin', a Hadlin' and the Tree, ain't there no more. Mamma took me ta 'em ta be falsely ascended. All 'cause I wanted ta be they Keeper and *you* didn't."

"No, that's not true. They accepted you." Pointing to the Hadling standing beside Brin, Veya pressed her point, "I witnessed it. This one fed. The link worked. You gave the stones in your bag to the Mortling, and the Hadling fed on them. That means whatever was wrong is fixed and makes you their Keeper. Doesn't it?"

"Oh, Veya, ya got no knowin.'"

"No knowing? I'm tired of hearing about your knowing, and Mamma's knowing. Is there another damn book I should be reading? I read the Keepers' book. Is there some ritual I have to go through? Tell me, tell me what to do, what else I need to know."

Brin wiped at her eyes. "A knowin' ain't in no books and it ain't somethin' I can just give ya. It's seein' how a thing works or doesn't. It's like knowin' when ta plant beans and when ta wait a spell. Oh, I know there be books on plantin' and such. But the knowin' I be talkin' on ain't always writ in a book. The old Keepers, they tried ta give us all they knowin'. But some things can't be writ. Some things got ta be felt. You understand?"

Veya nodded, because an understanding had finally dawned on her. Brin's *knowing* was nothing more than blind faith that an intuition would always show her the way to overcome any situation. But backwoods intuition wasn't what Veya wanted, what she desperately needed. She had to have cold, hard facts. The unsteady fear pursuing her turned to anger. Her rage built. A cold, harsh realization settled and blossomed—the awareness that her sister, with their mother's help, had led her down to a pit filled with creatures trapped in a Tree. Brin and their mother had no plan other than their blind faith in a goddamn *knowing* to save them.

Building behind the cloying fingers of fear, guilt, and panic encircling Veya was a thick wall of fury. She welcomed its presence.

Veya turned to unleash her newly found wrath on her sister, but the anguish reflected in Brin's eyes sent Veya's rage fleeing. Yet, now that she had unleashed it, it could no longer go back to hiding. So it settled within the familiar weighted folds of her anguish and grief.

Brin looked out at the Hadlings and Mortlings with an immense sorrow mirrored in her eyes. Veya had never witnessed such unfiltered grief in another human being. How could her sister's fragile frame contain such overwhelming sorrow? In Veya's attempt to understand she sorted through her knowledge base as a therapist, and in so doing realized her sister was holding more than sorrow in her being. When the label for what she was witnessing in Brin surfaced her stomach lurched. It couldn't be?

Love?

How, how could her sister *love* these creatures?

She tried to reconcile her revulsion with what she witnessed in her sister. But the very notion Brin could care so deeply for them was beyond Veya's comprehension. The idea seemed unfathomable, until a fleeting movement within a dark corner of the Tree, a glint of flowing red, caught her attention. That brief moment of anticipation, held for her an expectation of seeing the specter who wore the face of her Triste.

Her mind grasped her sister's pain—children.

Can Brin see these things as the children she can't have?

Veya strained to pull her tattered pieces of logic together as Brin began to speak, "I only done fixed the one Hadlin' and the one Mortlin' so they might help in gettin' us down here. I didn't even have a knowin' if it'd work. Ya got ta believe me when I say, *I* got no knowin' on how ta fix what really be broken here. I got some healin' in my bein', but it don't make me they Keeper."

Brin turned her heartbroken gaze from the ailing Mortlings and Hadlings to Veya. Her face wore a mask of pain Veya didn't recognize, nor had she ever heard Brin's voice so shrill and panic-stricken. "Mamma ain't talkin' ta me no more. She ain't talkin' ta me! Is she gone? Or has the voice talkin' ta me been a Hadlin's, a trap ta get us here?"

Veya recalled Hadlings had whispered dark things to humans in the Keepers' book on beginnings. She dismissed the ludicrous idea as the thought of their all-knowing mother being dead clutched her heart.

No, it's impossible. She and Triste are still alive.

"Answer me, Veya, is she …" Brin could not say the word, *dead.*

Veya looked to where the gleam of red fabric had momentarily wavered. No red, just a black, empty hole.

She tried to calm her sister. "I'm sure Mamma is fine. Remember Dr. Mary is with her. She'll see Mamma's taken care of."

Brin appeared not to have heard her, and Veya feared her sister was giving up. Her harsh words came out in a rush, "This is all your doing. Your's and Mamma's. Do you know why they took Mamma and Triste's stones? I know they're a protection, but you've never told me what the stones actually protect us from?" Veya lifted the stone from around her neck. It glowed so bright she couldn't look at it directly.

Brin's amulet also glimmered brilliantly. Above the stone her eyes had transformed, once again shining with their usual joy and optimism. Veya didn't stop to wonder why, as Brin answered her question. "Like I done told ya, Mamma says each a' our stones let us know when a Hadlin' or Mortlin' be near. It be ta protect us against Hadlins being able ta harm us. But most important she says the stones be a way a' keepin' the sorrow from settlin' too deep inside a' us. St. James women ain't like other folks who can shed sorrow over time. We be more inclined to take in the greivin' 'round us, and when it settles in us, we be in danger a' bein' eaten up by it. Never been the way with me. Mamma says it can't enter me 'cause I got the healin' gift. Once my stone was ripped from my neck by a child filled with pain from her mamma dyin' right 'afore her very eyes. The woman drowned in the bayou, while the child stood unable to help, knee deep in mud. I held on ta her sobbin' little body without my stone. Her sadness never once entered me. My own thinkin' is the stones also be a way for the Mortlins ta find us when they be needin' a St. James woman."

The tattered pieces were coming together for Veya. Each *knowing* provided another fragment toward finding what she so desperately needed, how to free Triste. She asked, "So the Hadlings were able to trap Triste, or whatever part of Triste is in that thing that looks like her, because she didn't have a stone to protect her? Is that why Triste's personality has changed these last few months?"

Caressing her stone, Brin replied, "That be what Mamma be thinkin'. It be why she sent Dr. Mary ta Triste."

The final piece fell into place as Veya cautiously asked, "If we get Triste's stone back, will the Hadlings release their hold on her?" An unresolved bit frayed the edges of Veya's brief moment of hope. "Why did they take Mamma's stone too? Couldn't she have helped them?"

The clicking of the Hadlings claws that had followed Veya for hours began again and increased in pitch, taking on the rhythmic cadence of a drum's beat. Click, click, click—click—click.

Brin spoke over the unnerving din. "Like I said, things ain't been right for some time, but when Mamma took me in to ascend is when the Mortlins stopped coming ta

Mamma for sorrow stones. It's why Mamma come out to the Tree the day I found her, and couldn't wake her."

Everything was falling into place, like stones falling from a pouch. "Dr. Mary said the Islanders were sick, and getting worse. How long have they been getting worse? Months, days?"

"Don't matter now."

The clicking increased in volume. Click, click, click …

Veya had to yell above it. "Yes, it does. I have to know if I could've stopped this."

"Would you've believed it, Veya? Even if I'd a'gone ta ya and begged ya ta come home, back to the Island?"

Veya started to say yes, of course. But she knew she never would've come back, never, if not for Triste.

"Now, I figure the Mortlins stopped coming ta Mamma cause she tried ta force 'em ta take me as they Keeper. The Hadlins, they was a starvin' so they trapped they kin down here in the Tree thinkin' they could force 'em ta feed 'em. But they couldn't 'cause Mortlins don't got no sorrow a' they own, and no stones ta give a Hadlin'. The Mortlins be needin' the Keeper ta give 'em the stones filled with human sorrows."

The tapestry of information Veya needed was almost complete. Brin moved in closer so she didn't have to yell as Veya motioned for her to keep explaining. "So the Hadlins be dyin' cause they got no sorrow ta feed 'em, and with no Hadlin' ta feed the Tree, the Tree be dyin' too. It be why the Tree got us all trapped. I guess they got no way a knowin' if they keep us down here, we gonna die and they goin' ta die right 'long with us. I'm sorry. I been a tryin' ta mend things, and now your Triste, and our mamma …" Tears flowed down Brin's cheeks as she covered her ears against the clicking.

A large group of Mortlings moved and gathered beside Brin. She took a Mortling's hand into her own before speaking to Veya, "I be a healer. I always knowed I be a healer. But even I can't heal this many. Can I?" The clicking ceased, as though doing her bidding, when Brin swept her hand to encompass the number of Mortlings and Hadlings that had begun moving out of the Tree's dark corners, and toward the heart center.

Brin and the Mortlings gathered beside her left Veya to join the multitudes at the heart center. But before she was out of her sister's hearing range Brin turned. Her face, even with its lines of age, no longer showed signs of anguish as she said, "The world be a mighty sorrowful place, and human beings be needin' all these Mortlins and Hadlins ta keep such overwhelmin' misery away. Without 'em, more a' the Islanders will be a'sufferin' along with the increasin' number a' land-walkers comin' ta give they sorrow stones ta Mamma. Mamma says there be more Sorrow Keepers in the world. I got no knowin' of it. What I am a wonderin' is where's all the sufferin' gonna settle when they be no way a' cleansin' it? Then there be your

Triste, and our mamma. Are they done dead? Am I too late?"

"Brin, stop, where are you going?" Veya went to follow her sister, but dozens of Hadlings blocked her way, forming a wall of dark, leathery beings. Their eyes glowed red while their claws tapped the small animal skulls hanging from their necks.

After placing the still pulsing stones she held in her hand back in the pouch, Veya successfully slid past the first Hadling. As she attempted to pass the second, a Hadling's hand wrapped around her wrist. Its sharp talon dug into her flesh. The harder she struggled to break through their wall of bodies, the more clawed hands wrapped around some part of her.

When the Hadlings finally released her, they were replaced by familiar ropes of panic tightening across her chest. She fought against it, as she continued to fight the impenetrable wall of beings. She screamed out. She yelled for Brin, for Triste, even for her mother. She screeched again and again until, with a voice ragged and hoarse, she fell limp. Their course hands were the only things preventing her fall.

The creatures had parted for Brin, allowing her to walk through them, and up to the onyx altar. Veya had a direct line of sight to her from where she stood trapped by the Hadlings at the head of the altar. To the right and left of the table, closely spaced oblong stone steps created a stairway to the top. Mortlings stood in a single line on either side of the stairway, leaving a path as though waiting for a procession to climb them. But it wasn't a procession. It was Brin, alone, who walked up to the altar.

Brin moved purposefully but slowly, her arms rising above her head, and her eyes lifting upward. As her galoshes made contact with each individual oval stair, she paused until a stone embedded in the oval burst with light. When she stepped from the last oval and onto the altar, the colors of each stone burned bright. Their colors were identical to the way stones they'd followed to reach the heart center.

Brin stood at the center of the altar and looked down on Veya.

The Hadlings' kept their blockade, preventing Veya from reaching her sister.

Brin once again reminded Veya of the Virgin Mary painting hanging on their mother's bedroom wall. But instead of a blue veil, Brin's red hair flowed wildly about her pale face. Hadlings climbed the Mortling-lined stairs, and began gathering at the foot of the rock altar.

Brin lowered her arms. Her gaze still locked on Veya, she said, "Mamma used ta say I be more like a Mortlin' than a Hadlin' since sorrow never rested in me for but one heart's beat. But then sorrow never before has rested in a Mortlin' even for a short breath a' time. So lately she been sayin' maybe I be more like a Hadlin'. She says it be 'cause

I got a healin' in me, and so do the Hadlins since they be the ones eatin' the sorrow and releasin' the grief from the stone's giver. Without the Mortlins and Hadlins could humans continue ta carry so much grief? And without human sorrows how would they and the Tree continue ta live?"

Veya tried again to shove and push her way through the wall of Hadlings, but to no avail.

Brin continued speaking, "I so wanted ta be they Keeper, but it ain't ta be. The sorrow what I never felt 'afore be a'flowin' in me now. It be settlin', and I got no way a' gettin' it out. I ain't never had such a heaviness, such a darkness, residin' in me 'afore. So, I done figured it Veya. I sorted how I can mend it. At least I got ta try."

The Hadlings standing directly behind Brin had closed their eyes, and their chests began opening. The Mortlings, their hands filled with stones, were surrounding Brin. They moved ever closer around her until they engulfed her. She disappeared, absorbed by a wall of leathery green and black bodies.

A sharp, burning, scream tore through Veya, cutting at her vocal cords.

"No! Brin!"

The chests of the Hadlings holding her captive began opening. Their trance-like state allowed her to escape.

When Veya reached the altar, a creeping fog floated on its surface, becoming denser the closer she got to the center. All around her ribbons of mist floated, as dozens of Mortlings held out stones, feeding the dozens of Hadlings whose chests were open and pulsating. At the center where a wall of Mortlings stood, bursts of bright white light shot out in tendrils, weaving their way upward. Veya pushed and shoved her way through until the Mortlings fell away, allowing her entry.

"Brin?"

Her sister lay on her back at the center of the altar, face up, her arms spread out. Once again the painting in their mother's room came to Veya, but this time Brin resembled not the Virgin Mary, but her son, the man nailed to the cross. It's where the resemblance ended, because her sister didn't look in pain or filled with sorrow.

Her sister's face shone with a joy so vibrant it radiated through the emerald green irises of her open eyes. Brin's crown of red hair spread out against the ebony altar looked like a river of flowing fire. She no longer wore her galoshes, and her naked feet glowed stark white. On every flat surface of her body a stone shimmered. From each stone bursts of the vapor feeding the Hadlings flowed. Any skin left uncovered on her sister's body glistened, resembling the inside of the crystal way stones.

Veya searched within herself for a small piece of the bliss and serenity bursting forth from her sister and found none.

Triste. Only Triste has ever created such happiness in me.

She knelt at Brin's side, caressing her face, and was astonished when Brin's lips parted in a smile, and her body shook with a laugh. The stones placed on her forehead and cheeks shifted position for a moment, and then lay flat once more.

It seemed to Veya that she and Brin remained there, wrapped in a circle of time never-ending while the tendrils cocooned them from what lay behind, and from the unknown of what lay ahead.

A rumble coming from beneath the altar broke the spell. Veya looked up to see the Hadlings' chests were closed. The beings no longer clung to each other for support. When she looked back down at Brin the tendrils evaporated in a gentle mist and were gone.

Brin's eyes were closed. Veya asked, "Is it done? Did you fix it? Where's Triste?"

But Brin's eyes remained closed. The age lines on her face were back, and joined by many more. Veya shook her sister. The stones falling from her were picked up by Mortlings.

The knot in Veya's stomach grew larger. It felt as though the Mortlings were taking the stones from Brin, and putting them into her, suffocating her.

She cried, "Brin! Wake up, you did it."

When her sister's eyes finally opened in narrow slits Veya's struggle for air ceased, and she took a full deep breath.

She's okay. It'll all be over soon.

Then Brin said, "It ain't done yet. Tell Mamma I love her, and Daddy too. Don't ya grieve for me, now. You'd a done the same—the same for your Triste."

Veya's heaviness increased tenfold and she struggled once more to breathe. "No, you can't. No! Don't leave me Brin."

She looked to the Hadlings and Mortlings for help, but they were descending the stairs from the altar. "Wait, she helped you, now you have to help her. Wait." She tried to grab at them, but her hands slid from their slick, scaly bodies. They continued to walk away until she and Brin were alone on the huge stone slab.

The bayou of tears Veya had held back, burst forth when she looked at her sister's tranquil face, and un-breathing body. Veya's stone, heavy on her neck, swayed between them, its glow throwing sparks of light on Brin's face.

No light emanated from Brin's stone.

Brin was dead. Their twin stones confirmed it.

"What am I going to do now? Where are Mamma and Triste's stones? Don't leave me alone, please." She cradled Brin to her chest. Wave upon wave of grief, and anger, crashed and fought for her attention. She heard the creatures going about their lives. Listened to the pounding of new stones in the Tree's bark. They'd shown no regard for Brin's death. She hated them now more than ever.

With Brin's head cradled in her lap, she cried until she had no more tears. Again and again she screamed and railed at the Hadlings and Mortlings, until finally drained, she lowered Brin's head onto the altar and lifted her own. Her chest and sides ached. "What do I do now?" she whispered to the still, serene body of her sister.

Have I lost Triste too?

She stood before realizing her only source of light was the lone stone hanging from her neck. The oval steps of the stairway no longer glowed. The white of the way stone at the Heart Center no longer shone.

The impenetrable void tightened around her, just as the ropes of a panic attack would. She inched toward where she thought the stairs would be, relieved to see an oblong step appear in the faint light cast by her small stone.

She descended the altar. Red eyes peered at her from out of the dark.

As she stood wondering where she would go, a cold claw grabbed at her arm. She jumped and yelled in anger, "Leave me be!"

A white light flashed to her right. A dim glow remained in its wake.

A way stone? Are they going to show me the way out?

Red, bright and flowing, rippled at the edges of the dim glow.

"Triste?"

A voice came to Veya in disjointed beats. "Yes—Mamma—I'm—Finally—Home."

Another flash of light revealed Triste sitting amongst a large group of Hadlings. Her eyes, her smile, gleamed like Brin's had. Triste radiated love—love of the dark beings surrounding her.

Veya's mind snapped and traveled back to the time when her mother had laid her on the altar and spoken the words Veya had carefully concealed in her grief and anger. It was the time Veya knew her mother had foretold that she, Veya, would become the Keeper after her mother died. She frantically tried to bury the words her mother had spoken again, but they would no longer be suppressed. What had been said ran through her veins like a plague, worse than anything her logical mind could've created. They sprouted from her memory like snakes filled with poison.

But they weren't the words Veya had feared. They were worse. Her mother had not said, "*You* will be the next Keeper." She'd said, "You will *birth* the next Keeper."

The words sprang, like snake venom seeping in her mind. Veya could not escape them. The cold, hard facts she so preciously clung to now spiraled her into a deep chasm draped in the layers of denial she'd used to shield herself.

Triste, I've lost you.

Veya fell to the ground. The weight of the bag of stones she'd placed back in her pocket brought her to her knees. She couldn't move. She had no will to move, no reason to move. She lay down on her side and curled in on herself.

Creatures scuffled around her. Their rat feet slid past her and still she did not move. A Hadling's face appeared inches from her own. Her eyes opened wide long enough to follow his pointing claw to a Tree root an arm's reach away.

With her knees pushed against her chest, her right cheek pressed to the ground, she reached in her pocket for the bag of stones. She intended to throw them at the Hadling. But as she lifted the bag and poured them in her hand the gravity of their weight baffled her. Each stone, heavier than the next, filled with an unearthly substance she could not fathom.

She sat up to study the small, yet weighty stones piled in the palm of her hand. A green one had been added. She knew the emerald stone held the sorrow of Brin's death. A deep despair pulled at her. She tried to lie down again, but the Hadling pricked her arm, and again pointed toward the Tree root.

"You want my damn stones? You have my sister, my brother, now—now you even have …" She couldn't say it, she wouldn't say … *Triste.*

She shoved the stones toward the Hadling. "Here, take them, take my damn sorrow." She had to use both hands in order to move the heavy pouch toward the creature. Their weight had increased.

The Hadling again pointed toward the Tree's root.

Her mamma's words from long ago, ricocheted through her mind. *Since you're a St. James woman, ya have ta give the Tree your sorrow yourself child.*

"Fine, you want my damn sorrow. Here!" She took the ruby, rose-etched stone from the bag given to her when her grandmamma died. Grabbing a larger stone from the ground she began pounding the ruby stone into the Tree's bark while reciting the words she knew she must say. The words contained the grief of a nine-year-old girl. "I will never again hear your calming voice when fear threatens to take me, or feel the comfort of your arms as they hold me in a tight hug." She threw the larger rock aside and pounded harder, using only the heel of her hand.

With her bloodied fingers, she reached for another stone. The gray crescent moon river stone.

"This is for my baby brother." She'd held this first sorrow the longest, and her brother's death tore through her like a knife cutting her from the inside. "I will never smell his sweet scent again or feel the soft down of his hair." She clawed at the Tree's root, breaking and splitting her fingernails to bury the stone deep in its bark.

Something shifted in her as she shoved the next stone—the emerald green of her sister's eyes—ever deeper in a crevice of the Tree's root.

The next, a smooth obsidian stone in the shape of a book, she realized held the sorrow of her love for Triste's father. She lifted her arm to throw the stone from her sight, but she didn't. Instead, she yelled out, "I will never have your love, or see the gleam in your eyes when you hold our child to your heart."

With each stone she remembered—remembered the sorrow she held so dear.

The final amethyst stone, she knew carried the grief she felt over never having the kind of mother she'd always wanted. "We've lost so much Mamma. I'm sorry there is no time left."

When all the stones were gone, she looked down to where she had placed them. They formed a perfect galaxy of their own, swirling along with the many others she'd seen surrounding the base of the altar.

Warm water pooled around her. She placed her bloodied hands in the liquid and sat mesmerized. The stones she'd placed appeared to move while red ribbons of her blood flowed through and over them.

Exhaustion overtook her. The whirls of water where she sat were captivating. Tinged by her blood, it seemed to serve as a looking glass into another world. A world where many more Trees grew below. Even as she sat on solid ground, she felt suspended in time and space. Had the Tree, the Mortlings, the Hadlings, or maybe all combined, given her the gift of seeing the underground world spoken of in the Keepers' book? Veya Marie St. James, for the first time in her life, didn't try to apply logic to what she saw, or felt.

The bag that had held her stones sat deflated beside her, empty. She too, sat empty, yet lighter somehow, her chest no longer plagued by constricting bands. She hoped now the creatures would let her lie down and die. Without the weight of the stones, she could stand, but instead stayed sitting, gazing at the spiral she'd created in the Tree's bark, and the mystical underworld of Trees below.

Something brushed against her face. She looked up to see a Hadling standing over her. She reached to push the horrid creature away, but before she could, it held out its clawed hand. Hanging from it were two necklaces, each with a glowing red stone. The Hadling placed them around her neck where her own stone shone and walked away.

She looked down at them—one white—two red— glowing bright—her stone, her mother's stone, and Triste's stone. The Hadlings, perhaps with the help of the Mortlings, had released Triste. A single tear escaped her eye for the sacrifice Brin had made.

The rumble she'd heard earlier coming from below the altar began again. As she stood the ground around her transformed.

Lights.

Lights were sparking everywhere she looked. Galaxies of stones swirled around her of their own accord, and not by some illusion of water flowing over them. She looked from the underworld below and as far as her vision would allow up through the hollow of the Tree. Her gaze traveled the Tree's inner wall as each way stone she and Brin had followed ignited and were joined by smaller sparks of colored lights resembling fireflies. The rainbow of lights formed a perfect spiral within the inside of the Tree, along the path the Mortlings, Hadlings, and Keepers had created down to the heart center.

Looking up toward the top of the Tree and the radiant spiral of stones along the way, it was impossible to calculate or fathom the distance she and Brin had trudged down.

When Veya finally tore her eyes from the spiraling path, the cause of the rumble revealed itself as a hole opening beyond the altar, at the far end of the Tree's base.

A way out?

Past the altar, a path of luminous way stones lit up one by one to lead her to the opening. She wouldn't have to climb back up, and even though her previous exhaustion had evaporated she was thankful. Because she had a *knowing* when she left the Island and returned to Ashland Triste would be awake.

Her *knowing* came from not just a St. James' woman's instinct. It was also confirmed by the one white, and two ruby red necklaces vibrantly alive, and glowing at her chest.

A Mortling came to stand beside Veya. No longer the swamp rat of her nightmares, its luminescent skin radiated as though covered in droplets of iridescent liquid. She reached out and took its hand. Mortlings lifted Brin from the altar and carried her toward the Tree's now fully-opened entrance. Yet even as Brin's body left the tree, Veya knew her sister's spirit would forever remain with the Mortlings and Hadlings—her children.

Hadlings stood as sentries on either side of the opening. Buoyant, Veya's foot hit the first tourmaline tinged way stone leading out of the Tree. Her mind counted—*one*—then went no further. Her feet alighted, weightless on each consecutive stone until she stepped out of the Tree and passed through the Andirons.

I'm coming, Triste.

The writing bug first snagged Cheryl Owen-Wilson through the penning of a personal essay, for which she received an award and publication. Today what drives her writing life is Southern Gothic fiction. Since her biological roots are buried not only in Oregon but deep in the bayous of Southern Louisiana, the genre is a natural fit.

When not writing she can be found at an easel covered in oil paint. "When I write I usually have a painting in mind. The same holds true when a painting forms—a story generally follows." One of her paintings is featured on the cover of *ShadowSpinners: A Collection of Dark Tales.* You can find her short story, *Swamp Symphony,* in the book's collection. *Bayou's Lament* is Cheryl's first published novella.

**Complete Rulebook
&
Labyrinth of Souls Tarot Deck**
Available at
matthewlowes.com/games

Labyrinth of Souls Fiction
Coming Soon

The Ruptured Firmament by Stephen T. Vessels

Aftermath by Cythia Coate-Ray

... and more to come!

information at

shadowspinnerspress.com

www.ingramcontent.com/pod-product-compliance
Lightning Source LLC
Chambersburg PA
CBHW021655110726
47902CB00007B/1939